The Warding
Of
AnnaBella Cain

Kefira Zink

The Warding Of AnnaBella Cain

The Chronicles of AnnaBella Cain Book Two

The Warding of AnnaBella Cain
Copyright ©2025 by Kefira Zink

Contact Info: kefirazinkauthor@gmail.com

ISBN: 979-8-9928400-0-1

Table of Contents

Book One: Fracture   6

Book Two: Healed   143

Book One: Fractured

Bella Part One

As I closed the folder on another life, my right arm started to hurt again. No, not hurt. Hurt was not really the right word for what I felt, but it is the best word I had for it. I held my arm up so I could look at it. There, running from my wrist to my elbow was the thin, pinkish line, ruler straight, that was my punishment. Like I had done a thousand times, I traced that small line, feeling the slight puckering of the scar, remembering everything that had happened a hundred years ago on the first day of summer break from school when I was seventeen.

My father had revealed to me who he was that summer. Satan to some, other names to others. He had told me that the gods of every religion in the world that ever had or ever would exist were real and were all serving together on a Commission that ruled life as we knew it. Dad wasn't a bad man, or evil. He was just the man who told your sins to the god of your choosing so they could judge your life after you died and determine if you were to be punished or rewarded. He asked me to join him, to become like him, a servant to the gods, a coordinator. I agreed to try and went to the Trials Arena to test my Heka, my level of power that created everything, was everything.

And I passed. Better than passed. I did the twelve tests better than almost everyone, ever. I had been good in school, so I expected to do well at these Trials too, but I never expected to do that well. And I never expected what happened next. The gods were not happy with my Trials. Not because I did so well, but because my father never applied for permission to have a child with a human. Because I used the Heka, the power that made the gods, humans and everything else, in a way they didn't know was even possible. Because the Heka, the entity that is the noncorporal embodiment of that power, spoke to me during the Trials when It never had spoken to anyone before. Because the gods didn't know the Heka could speak to people at all.

So, I was put through a criminal trial and the gods condemned me for what I couldn't control, saying I misused the Heka and that I broke the rules of the Trials because humans and human-coordinator hybrids were not allowed to take the test anymore. The gods treated me like a human and had Malachi, an ancient human working for the gods, use his special ability to determine what my real faith was. Malachi was the examiner of faiths. He could know a person's true faith at a glance and used this ability for all humans on trial at the end of their lives to make sure they were judged by their real faith accurately. Malachi told them I did not follow any gods, but had faith in humans to govern themselves, which he was probably right about.

The Speaker of the Commission of the Gods decided the best thing to do was let humans decide my fate. She gave them a choice of punishments for me: human and no memory of anything that had happened or coordinator with no ability to ever go to earth again, my human mother believing I had died. Those who read my story must have chosen coordinator because I was released from my prison, and the implant put in my arm. I don't know how they put the implant in. All I remember is one moment I was lying on the bed in my cell, bored and the next I was waking up in the hospital wing of the prison, my right arm sore and heavily bandaged, with Malachi sitting quietly next to me. He said the gods had deemed that I was a flight risk, so the implant was necessary to dampen my Heka, make It only as strong as I would need to work with my father. And the implant bound me to the heavenly realms. For eternity.

He said I would forget the implant was there after a time. That I would forget about my human life. Every once in a while, though, I could still feel it. A twinge running through my arm. The warm over cold that the Heka had felt like back in the Trials running up my arm, but It stopped short of going any further. He said I would forget, but I never did.

"Bella," a man said behind me. I had forgotten where I was, tracing my scar and remembering. The man laid a gentle hand on my shoulder and I turned to look at him. It was my father, Nick Cain. Tall, lean, muscular, with dark eyes and wavy hair, a Spanish air to him with just a hint of an accent, Dad always looked impressive in a suit. Before that summer, I had never seen him in suit, only faded band tees and relaxed jeans, sun glasses perched on his head and driving a cool car. Now, I could hardly remember him like that. At least I got to see his face often enough to remember him well. My mom was a distant, fading memory. A feeling of her hugs and the scent of blooming flowers was all I had left.

My dad had still been speaking as my mind wandered, "Bella, you can go home now. It's my shift." I looked around. We were in a courtroom, not too different from the ones back home, that humans used every day. We were in a small room with two large wooden tables, one to the right side and one to the left. I was seated at the one to the left, the prosecutor's table, in a plush office chair that face a large wooden raised bench, like any judge would sit at. Except this judge's bench had one difference. It could expand and contract as needed. If a person's faith had many gods and goddesses, the bench would expand to let them all sit there during a trial. If there was only one god or goddess, the judge's bench would shrink back down to a normal size.

In front of the other table, the defense's side, there was another bench, smaller than the judge's but bigger than ours. That is where Malachi sat. For the dead humans that came into this room, Malachi had the innate power to tell what their true faith was, whether it be the one they professed to believe while they were alive or not, and call the gods of that faith to the courtroom to judge their life. There was a door behind his bench that would appear after a trial was over, and the gods had made their ruling. Malachi would lead the newly dead through that door to face whatever came next for them, whether it be heaven, hell, reincarnation, or whatever else the gods had chosen for them.

As the prosecutor, it was my job to understand every religion and know what was considered right and wrong by that belief's rules. With my Heka, what little I was allowed, I would know the basics of that faith, and would know that person's life at a glance. I would tell the gods where they had gone wrong while they were alive, and it was the human's job, or their defender's if they had one, to explain how they got things right enough to overlook that. Dad did the same job as me. The only time I saw him anymore was when we switched who was on duty or if there was some sort of mass issue with the humans that led to an overflow of newly dead to be processed.

The implant was not foolproof. I still had some human to me no matter what they tried. I still sometimes got tired and needed to sleep, or hungry and needed to eat. Most of the time, I wouldn't even notice these human needs until they were urgent, or until Dad came to relieve me. Then the feelings of a full bladder, exhaustion and a grumbly stomach would hit me hard. Since time works kind of wonky here, I was never sure if I was going hours or days between times of humanness. But somehow Dad always knew when he was needed.

Most coordinators and gods hadn't ever needed those human needs. They may have participated in them for fun, but never out of need. Most demi-gods remembered those from when they were human, and maybe enjoyed to still eat or sleep for fun. And the humans here? Well, they were dead so what they needed, I am not sure, but they would also eat and sleep sometimes. But the gods could not fix that AnnaBella Cain was at least partly a living human, and always would be, so they had to allow me to be human and have time off. So that is when Dad worked. When I needed time off to be human.

Dad spoke again, this time a little concerned, "Bella? You ok?" He tenderly pulled on my shoulder to turn me towards him.

I didn't want to worry him, so I spoke a little too quickly. "Sure, yeah, just tired I think," I covered. Dad raised an eyebrow as if to say he wasn't sure he believed me, but I smiled to hide the lie, and gave him a quick hug. Dad had been punished for having me by being banned from the human realm for a thousand years. Sometimes I think he worried that the living human part of me would get sick or hurt and he wouldn't have any way to fix it. So, I hid that the implant hurt sometimes from him.

We never talked about the pain and needing human time. We also never talked about the trial, my punishment and the fact that it was kinda all his fault yet I was the only one who was really punished for it either. Well, me and Mom. Dad lied to me. He never told me, or Mom, that having a child with a human was banned. He also never told me that I wasn't supposed to do the Trials. Yeah, he was punished for his actions by being banned from the human realm, but that didn't bother him very much because the only person he would really miss from the human realms is me.

But he didn't lose me. I was the one who actually had people to miss there, like Mom. And, Mom? She got spent the rest of her life thinking that her child had died, and that wasn't fair to her either. Sometimes, I think he acts the way he does, too kind and concerned, because he is scared that I will decide to be angry enough about all this stuff that he caused by his lie, and decide never to speak to him again or something. I am angry at him, or at least I was, but over time my anger has diminished some. There were points in those first few years where I wanted to yell at him, and sometimes I swore I would never talk to him again even.

But then I noticed that, when I let my anger at Dad build up too much in me, I would end up being too hard on the humans I was judging. In my frustration at Dad, I would point out the tiniest mistakes they had made in their life and push punishments that they really didn't deserve. So, I had to let my anger subside. I could have been the evil everyone thought this job was, but that would have been wrong. Humans are flawed and I can't blame them for their flaws for eternity just because I am having a bad day. The gods expect me to be fair in my decisions about what mistakes actually should be held against a human, not petty. So, I let go of my anger at Dad for the humans' sake, and justice's. Well, mostly let it go.

I also hid that my implant hurt from the gods because who knows what they would do if they knew.

I stood up and stretched, then gathered the stack of files that represented every deceased human whose life I had helped judge today. I am short, only 5' 3", and the workload had been heavy, so I had to look to the side of the stack of files in my arms because I couldn't see over it. The door at the back of the courtroom opened and a woman walked in, looking nervous. The next case was coming in. It was time for me to leave. As the woman walked up to the defendant's desk, I said goodbye to Dad, walked back down to the door she had come in and went out into the hallway.

Instinctively, I turned to the right, refusing to look to my left. I knew that down that way was the silver door that led to the full Joint Commissions Room, the room where all the gods, goddesses, and demi-gods met to make the rules the whole world had to follow. It is also where they put me on trial after I completed the Trials Arena. I never wanted to see that door again, but was forced to walk by it every day for the rest of eternity.

To the right instead, I walked down a short hallway that looked like any other office hallway, into a waiting room like any other waiting room, except this one was full to the brim with people from all walks of life, speaking every language. Some were sobbing, some happy. All of them recently deceased humans waiting to go before their gods for judgement.

I ignored the crowds and went to the reception desk. Hoisting my stack of files, I handed them to Jim. "Here are the completed cases for storage," I told him. "You know the humans have the technology to do all of this electronically. At least, when I was last there, they did. I bet it's even better now. Ever think about sending someone to check that out?"

Jim, a ruddy looking man with blond hair that would have passed for human, looked up and, ignoring my statement, asked in his deep southern drawl, "Going to the Annex again?" Jim took the files as he spoke to me.

"Yeah," I told him, slightly weary, "How will I learn it all if I don't study?"

Jim laughed and waved me off, taking the files behind his desk and turning away from me. The Annex was a building that contained the exact blueprint for every religion, faith, or belief system ever invented, sort of like a library for religions. No one was sure exactly how the Heka made the gods and goddesses that humans were drawn to believing in, but what they did know is that if humans at any time in the past, present or future believed in a god, the Heka made sure that god existed. Once they existed, the gods got to decide how their religion worked, what the details of it were, what the rules were and what punishments and rewards they would give out to believers. No god could break the Joint Commission rules, like gravity, but they could do occasional one-off miracles that seemed to be exceptions to those rules. Other than that, they were free to create what they wanted, including creation and origin myths, heavens and hells, and end-of-the-world doomsday prophecies at will.

Dad knew the exacts of each and every one of these beliefs, from the ones back when cavemen just discovered fire to the ones no one would believe in for another thousand years. He was Heka made, not human born. Even the human born demi-coordinators and demi-gods knew this stuff in a blink. But they put an implant in me to control my Heka. So, I had to study and learn it the old-fashioned way. And I thought senior year would be hard... Ha, it has lasted a hundred years so far and I'm only halfway through the Annex.

The ride down the elevator from floor 333, where the courtrooms are, to the lobby was fairly short, but that was all the time it took for my human hunger to kick in. Time didn't work quite right in this place, so sometimes I would get out of work and be starving, like I hadn't eaten in days. Which, honestly, could have been true in human time. What seemed like a normal eight-hour workday in the courtroom, may have actually been a week or a month, or ten minutes, in the human realm. I knew from when I broke time in the Trials Arena that time is connected in all the different places, the heavens, the human world, whatever, but that doesn't mean it plays by rules the rest of us understand. It's not a joint Commission type thing, and no one was really sure if it is a Heka thing or not. Basically, we all just accept time's randomness and just move on.

Once in the lobby of the building, I headed to the main doors, passing several cubicles and offices along the way. The building the courtrooms were in was called Central Hub. This was the main building where most gods and coordinators worked. There were other places they worked, including the Annex. Even in the hundred years I had been here, I had not learned them all, or all the jobs that coordinators could have.

Looking to my left as I walked down the hallway, I saw Bob was packing up to leave for the day too. Bob was Dad's friend from Accounting, and he and I had gotten to know each other over the time

I had been stuck here. I never really did learn how Dad and Bob became friends, or even what Bob's status was, coordinator or god. He was rather unpleasant to be around when he didn't have enough caffeine. But Bob had an energy drink in his hand, so instead of full-on flaming from head to toe, and screaming, he just had a little trail of smoke coming from the top of his head.

"Hey Bob," I called out, "headed out?"

Bob looked my way and waved, "Yeah, Bella. You?"

"Thinking a little Thai food sounds good," I replied, chuckling a little, "you want to join me?"

Bob chuckled and smiled sarcastically at me. Whichever he was, he never needed to eat, but did enjoy indulging in food from time to time. "Not tonight, darlin'," he said, shaking his head, "even the smell of spicy Thai food gives me heartburn, and I don't need anything else on me burning."

This was a running joke between us. Bob and I smiled at each other and went our own ways. I went on to the front door of the building and pulled out a small plastic badge. The door to the office building could be unlocked to go anywhere you needed, as long as you had the right door pass key. My father used a white one when he took me to and from home with the humans before I did the Trials and a green one to get to Area One where the Trials Arena was located. My pass key was red. This allowed me into the heavenly realms where all the coordinators and gods lived and worked. Sometimes humans were given the ability to stay in the Red Area as a reward from the gods for good and faithful lives. Based on my punishment rules, I was not allowed to apply for any other door keys.

I waved my red door key in front of the door, pulled the door open, and stepped outside into brilliant sunshine. Just outside the office door, I stopped for a moment. All this time and the way this city looked still caught me off guard.

The city that was the Red Area was named Taikarlu and it was huge and beautiful. Stepping out onto the sidewalk was like stepping out into any large, over-populated city. There were skyscrapers all around, lining the road in every direction. There were, well let's call them people for the sake of convenience, everywhere. In truth, they could be gods, demi-gods, coordinators, the souls of people who had passed on, the children of gods and coordinators who had heavenly privileges, or oracles and other humans who had been gifted in a special way by the Heka. But calling them all people is easier. These people were all over, some alone, others in groups, some moving slowly, enjoying the sights. Other were obviously busy, pushing past the sight-seers brusquely.

There were a few very noticeable differences between Taikarlu and cities like London, or New York City, or L.A. For one, there were no cars. Everyone was walking, or flying if they had wings. For another, the streets were made out of glass bricks. They looked just like cobblestone roads except each individual cobble was clear and reflected the light of the bright sun in prisms of rainbows in the air. The prisms of color would then reflect off the buildings that were made of gold. The whole atmosphere seemed to shimmer with light and color.

It was never not sunny in Taikarlu. No matter where you went, or when, the sun was always at its apex, shining right down on you. The weather in Taikarlu was also different. Where you went within the city determined what weather you experienced. In the Business District, where I lived and worked, it was always a beautiful summer day, not too hot, but just right. In the Old Town section, where most of the gods lived, it was perpetually spring. Sometimes there would be spring rain showers there, or even full thunderstorms. Even then, though, the sun would shine through the storm. There was more of a fall feeling in the River Run. As the name probably made you guess, there was a river that ran through this part of town that was full of fish. Crisp days with the smell of apple cider pretty much was the standard there, and everyone loved to spend time fishing in the river or running on the wooded trails. Most of the people who lived there were, or had originally been before they died, human. Then there is the Hills. This area was snowy and was where everyone went for winter fun. There were a few people who lived in the Hills but they were the exceptions who just liked winter better than wherever their type of people usually lived.

Then there was the Wastes. No one lived in the Wastes, not

anymore. I heard rumors that the Wastes used to be beautiful. One story I heard said it was where the gods held fire before it was gifted to humans. But they lost control of fire somehow and the Wastes became an oppressive desert no one dared go to anymore. It was kind of weird to me that, in a land created for the gods, who could create anything they wanted, they left the Wastes alone and wouldn't go there. I tried to ask about it once or twice, but stopped trying when everyone got super uncomfortable and would suddenly remember something they forgot to do somewhere else.

The amazement wore off after a second. I took a deep breath and turned to walk down the street towards my apartment. I wanted to change before I ate and headed to the Annex. I hated the clothes I had to wear when I was working. After the gods implanted me, I was released and given an apartment. Apparently, in Taikarlu, the economic system was kind of loose. Everyone just did the job they were created for and in return had an endless supply of their needs and wants filled.

Once the order came down that I was staying in Taikarlu as a coordinator, my father had been given a chance to explain how some things work in my new home and also train me for my job, since it was the same as his. Dad had explained the economy in a way that really didn't make sense. He said that the gods and coordinators really had no choice but to do what they did, their jobs. They were created by the Heka for that specific job and that was just who they were. No one would have a job they didn't like, because the job was created specifically for them and them for the job. So, everyone did their job without complaint. Since they weren't human, no one wanted more than they really needed or was fair for them to take, so there was no need to moderate what people had or got.

He never really did explain where the materials for the stuff came from in the first place, like where the wheat for bread or bricks for building houses came from. Coordinators like Dad, and all the gods, had been around for so long, I think they didn't question things like that anymore, or maybe they knew the answer and Dad just didn't think to tell it to me. Maybe, since I was the first demi-anything in a long time, he forgot that humans would question things just magically being there. Maybe it was another one of those things that most of the people in Taikarlu just knew, but I had to learn.

Either way, since I am still some level of basic human and the implant blocks my full information access, I really don't understand the full workings here. Gods and coordinators will take 'vacations' but it doesn't affect the everyday workings since time is such a messed-up thing. They don't get sick, so that's not an issue. But I still have my normal, teenage wants, needs or whatever, so I guess I can't really get not wanting anything but what you were made to want or need.

That is another thing that Dad tried to explain while training me but never really could in a way I understood. Why was I still at least partly human? In the past, when gods or coordinators had children with humans all the time, they knew how to make someone who passed the Trials fully god, demi-god or coordinator with no human limitations. But for some reason they couldn't do that with me. I had wondered if they had forgotten how over the millennia since they were allowed to have children with humans, but Dad had said that wasn't it. He said it had something to do with limits of Heka and the punishment I received, and that my humanness would fade in time, but, like I said, it didn't make any sense.

So, after they gave me the implant, I was assigned an apartment to live in. Not with Dad. Apparently, they were worried we would hatch some plan or something to defy our punishments, so we were not allowed to live anywhere near each other. I was given a bunch of clothes too. Work clothes. Stuffy suits. Humans who had died, it was explained, were under enough stress. It was comforting to see the people running the afterlife dressed in the ways they expected people of power to be dressed. So that meant well-tailored suits, dress shoes, the whole nine yards, just like my mom had worn to courtrooms when I lived with her. I guess it makes sense that if you had just died and saw the prosecuting attorney in the courtroom where your eternal life was to be judged, you wouldn't be comfortable if she looked like she was seventeen years old and wore ripped jeans and sneakers.

I walked down the streets, turning left and right as I needed to get to my apartment building. There were no street signs. One of those fun Heka tricks was that everyone who resided in Taikarlu knew where they were in the city at all times and how to get where they wanted to go without even thinking about it. There was no need for street signs or directions anywhere, everyone just had built-in GPS. Luckily, I got that Heka trick too. As I walked, the buildings around me changed from the skyscrapers to more moderately sized buildings.

My building was about halfway down a quiet street. It was brick with concrete steps up to the main double doors, just like brownstone townhouses in New York City. I went in and went to the third door off the main lobby. Home. Well, kind of. My apartment was a one-bedroom, nicely but plainly furnished. It was different than any other apartment in the building though, and apparently had given the housing people quite the issue. My partly humanness meant I actually needed a real bedroom, with a bed, as well as a kitchen and a bathroom. In a place where everyone else was either a god, coordinator, or dead, plumbing was never really needed before. They had plumbing and whatnot elsewhere, like in buildings where human guests might be brought in by some god or another, and in the jails where I was held before and after my trial. But they never thought about that being needed in the places where the residents of Taikarlu stayed, called their homes before because nobody had needed it before. I guess providing me with running water and a sewer system gave the gods running the place a bit of a headache. Oh well, they chose this, not me.

Once I got in my apartment, I kicked off the annoying shoes in the living room and quickly went to the bedroom to change into more comfortable clothing. My living room was only furnished with a couch and a TV. One benefit of living here? I got every single channel of cable from every country in the world and every streaming app free, no commercials, no ads, all the time. I never lost reception or had anything blocked or demonetized. Not that I watched television much. I usually was working in the Central Hub or studying at the Annex, so I wouldn't have time.

Over in the corner, near the kitchenette, was a large table that could seat eight. Mostly, the table was covered with maps of Taikarlu and the rest of the areas that were included in the heavenly realms, as well as documents about different religions, the history of the formation of the heavenly realms and other stuff I was trying to teach myself that most normal coordinators just knew automatically. One corner of the table was empty so I actually had somewhere to eat. The kitchenette was just the back wall of the living room, a couple of cupboards, a two-burner oven, sink, mini-fridge and microwave. I had added a coffee pot and an open shelving unit to store dry food in.

All the furniture and dishes had been in the place when they assigned it to me, and was all in various shades of blue. Tim, the maintenance guy, said if I didn't like what was in the apartment, I could get it swapped out for stuff I did like. Blue is an okay color, so I didn't bother. The only thing I did request was an area rug. The mahogany hardwood flooring was beautiful, but felt cold. I didn't expect some beautiful antique looking Oriental rug in blues and creams when I asked for the rug, but that's what Tim brought. Actually, he brought two. A matching set for the bedroom and living room.

The bedroom, besides the floors and rug, were as plain as the living room. One queen sized bed with, you guessed it, a bedspread and throw pillows in shades of blue. I had added a nightstand on one side of the bed, an alarm clock, lamp and a bookshelf to the room's décor. And the aluminum foil over the window, which freaked Tim and my neighbors out a little. The sun shines perpetually in Taikarlu. Blackout curtains only work so well, and I, as an almost human, really needed a good night's sleep. Luckily, Google still works here on a sort of basic level and one quick search on the library computer gave me that winner of an idea to block the sun so I can sleep at 'night'.

Oh, I should mention. Tim is the only other non-god, coordinator, or dead person I have met here. Actually, Tim is not one person. TIMS stands for Tangible Improvement Management Systems and is the complex system of maintenance, cleaning and repair robots that work in Taikarlu and the rest of the heavenly realms. Silver robots shaped like humans with only a passing resemblance to a face that can hear and talk. Their computer systems work like a hive mind. When something breaks anywhere in Taikarlu, the closest Tim gets assigned out to fix it immediately. All the TIMS have working rotations to keep everywhere clean inside and outside every building in Taikarlu. Beyond that, they help supply needs or do tasks when asked by any resident of the city. The TIMS are weirded out by me doing my own laundry and washing my own dishes. They don't get why I would need to do that, let alone why I do it instead of leaving it to them. The TIMS don't understand the concept of leftovers, or things still being usable when they are even the littlest bit worn or damaged, and will just throw out my food or clothes if I let them clean for me. I lost two perfectly broken in pairs of sneakers that way.

There are two doors in my bedroom as well. One is just my closet, which is a super large walk-in. Apparently, gods and other beings here like a lot of clothes and shoes and stuff, so they need tons of space to store them. I mean, I guess that makes sense for the gods. They can get offerings from their worshippers and, well, people love to gift clothes and jewelry. But for me the closet is mostly wasted space. Beyond my work clothes, which is just five identical pants suits, I really only wear jeans, t-shirts and hoodies. Which frustrates everyone here in Taikarlu a ridiculous amount. They can't understand why someone with access to every name-brand everything ever made would want to settle for a pair of skinny jeans ripped in the knees and an oversized black t-shirt that says, "In my defense, I was left unsupervised." I threw those clothes on, knowing that if I ran into Metis, my neighbor and a goddess not worshipped in a while on Earth, she would huff at me.

The other door in my room leads to a bathroom. It was a hastily constructed affair with a shower, ok water pressure I guess, toilet, sink and one of those European style washer-dryer combo deals. I stopped in there quickly just to take my hair from its professional up-do twist to a basic ponytail. My hair, being its brownish, barely curly, mess usually didn't last long in such fancy hairdos, so it took a minute to comb out the three pounds of hairspray I had used to tame it.

That done, I headed out of the bedroom and back into the living room. As I walked out the bedroom door, the world seemed to spin. A pain radiated up my right arm and everything went black.

"Stand back guys," Mrs. Campbell
said.

*The boys laughed again and started to
pull out their phones.
"If y'all even think about recording
her, you will be suspended, I guarantee
it," Mrs. Campbell's warning made
them stop pulling out their cellphones
but didn't stop their laughter.
"Anna?" I felt a hand touch my
shoulder, shaking it gently. "Anna,
can you hear me, sweetie?"*

When the world righted itself, I was lying on the floor, half in my bedroom, half out. It was not the first time I had passed out since becoming a coordinator, and definitely not the first time I had had a vision of myself in the human realm. It was another one of those things that happened when my arm hurt too much, but I never told anyone about. Fortunately, it had never happened around anyone else so I never had to try to explain it either. Since I was too scared to ask about my arm hurting, or by extension, the passing out, I always just chalked it up to the time issue and not knowing exactly how to work my body properly here.

I convinced myself that I must have been hungrier than I thought. Low blood sugar making me delusional. When I felt less shaky, I went into the kitchenette and found a granola bar to scarf down before heading out to find some real food. Then I found my shoes, my sneakers not those dreaded dress shoe abominations, slipped them on and headed out the door.

In the hallway of the building, Metis was waiting. I swear that woman has it out for me. It was like she had heard me come home and came into the hallway to wait, purposefully, just to have another chance to sneer at me.

"Are the TIMS malfunctioning?" She asked me.

Knowing her intent was not good, I ignored her and kept walking but she followed me to the door of the building.

"You know they will mend those clothes, right?" She continued, one lip of her perfectly Grecian sculpted face curling up in a sneer.

17

"Or you could get new ones that look decent. I mean if you insist on wearing jeans like some indigent, at least you could have the decency to wear ones that are well tailored."

Just keep walking, Bella, I told myself. One of these days I was gonna lash back at that woman and let her have it. But not today, I thought. Today I need to eat and get some work done at the Annex before exhaustion kicks in.

Metis didn't follow me out of the building, fortunately. Back out in the sunshine and beautiful day (maybe night, who knows?), some of the remaining bits of off-kilter I felt went away. Once I hit the main road, I decided I wanted to have gyros for dinner. Turning left towards the restaurant with the best gyros ever would take me the same direction as I would need to go to get to the Annex anyway. As I walked, I became curious.

Why were there so many restaurants in a place where no one actually needed to eat? Why did they even have apartments? I started thinking about the whole setup of Taikarlu and none of it made sense. I had accepted things as they were but would sometimes think about the fact that none of these people here, the gods and coordinators, needed stuff. But yet they had them. They all had them. Coordinators would work their jobs for only some hours, like a normal nine to five business day thing, then go home. But they are their jobs. They were created solely to do them, why would the Heka make them need to take breaks if they don't need to eat or sleep? And if they don't need breaks, why would they take them?

This wasn't the first time I thought about this in a hundred years. Every time I let my mind wander down this path, though, I always got stymied and had to forget it, saying someday I would make a friend I could ask. But making friends to talk to here had not been easy, for a lot of reasons. I realized, though, that I could never really understand everything here, everything I was attempting to learn at the Annex, unless I understood that part too. I would need to find someone willing to talk to me.

Arriving at the gyro place, I set the questions aside, and went in for my food. Markus, the owner of the restaurant saw me and hollered out, "Ah, Bella!"

Markus was a cool guy. He was human once and had always wanted to own a restaurant and make amazing food for people, food that made people happy. He never got to because his little brother had been born sick and, instead of doing what he wanted with his life, he went to work at a very young age to help his family pay for the treatments. When he was old enough, he worked hard in the place he lived to fight for better healthcare so no family would have to struggle like his did. So, when he died and his life was judged, I was the prosecuting attorney and it was pretty much open and shut as a good one, his gods decided to reward him with not only living in Taikarlu but getting the restaurant he always wanted.

"Bella," he continued, "lamb gyro, no tomato, and fresh fries, extra tzatziki on the side to dip the fries in, yes?" I nodded. This man knew all his customers' favorite orders, not just mine. Markos repeated the order to the kitchen, adding, "the fresh lamb, agoria, the fresh for Bella." Markos always thought that he got rewarded so well because of me. No matter how many times I told him it was his own choices in life that had let him have such a good death, he would always say, "I am not perfect person, you know. You know and say nothing that I am not perfect. I get good because of you, you eat good because of me, that's all," and would never let me talk anymore about it. I guess there were some nice perks to my job.

Markus brought me my food and I decided to eat while I walked to the Annex. It was a short walk, but plenty of time to eat a gyro. The fries, I would save for a snack for later. As I walked, I continued thinking. Maybe there were restaurants because of people like Markus. The gods and coordinators didn't need to eat, but how could they reward Markus with his dream unless there were people to eat there? I walked slowly, pondering this and eating the best gyro in any world.

I finished eating just as I arrived at the Annex. Before I entered, I found a Tim and gave him my leftovers. "Take this bag to my apartment, please. Just set it on the table, but not on the maps on the table." I asked it. "Oh, and do not clean while you are there. Nothing is to be moved, just leave the bag and do nothing else, ok?" I always had to add that part if I sent a Tim to my place without me. I didn't want to lose anymore shoes.

The Tim nodded, "Yes, Bella."

"Thank you," I replied. The Tim looked at me curiously and I just waved it away. Whoever programed the TIMS did not add pleasantries like please and thank you into its vocabulary, so they got confused when I said that every time. Even knowing that, I couldn't break the habit of being polite. Metis said it was like thanking the trash can, but they looked human enough that I just still said it instinctively.

Once the Tim left, I turned to the Annex. The outside looked rather unimpressive. It was a squat brick building, only one story high, with a small brass sign to the right of the plain glass door that said "Annex." It stood out on a street full of towering glass and gold buildings because it was so plain.

I waved my red card to unlock the door and went in. Walking through the door, the first thing I always noticed was the dusty smell. Everywhere else in Taikarlu smelled clean. Everywhere else, there were either flowers perfuming the air, or TIMS scrubbing everything all the time so that all you could smell was wood polish, or just a fresh, just cleaned, almost antiseptic smell. But the Annex was not cleaned by the TIMS. Too many ancient documents were kept there to trust the TIMS. The Annex-keeper and I were very much alike in that way. We didn't trust the TIMS because they never understood how something used could still be valuable.

Not that many people valued the Annex. Gavya, the coordinator who worked as the Annex-keeper, had told me the first time I came there that she hadn't seen another person, god, or coordinator in about three hundred years. Why would she? Most of them knew all the knowledge contained within the Annex automatically from the Heka. The only people who would normally have needed to go there were humans who were gifted and allowed to visit, like oracles or prophets. But there hadn't been any new oracles or prophets for several hundred years, or at least not any brought to live in Taikarlu without dying first. I was an anomaly.

The Annex looked small from the outside, but actually the building was narrow and long. Every square inch inside was covered with a maze of floor to ceiling bookshelves, all except the center of the building, where Gavya sat most of the time. There, a round desk commanded a view of the whole Annex. One side of the desk had a computer that Gavya could use to check out material. On the other side was an old-fashioned card catalogue that was the reference for finding anything in the Annex and a small spot with a chair for someone to sit and read.

The bookshelves on the Annex were bursting with old rolled up manuscripts, books, pictures and maps. There were photographs and reliefs of stone cave wall carvings, copies of mosaics from temples and pyramids, and hieroglyphics written on parchment made out of sheep skin. Basically, if the human world had written, drawn, or in any way made a notation of something about the gods or heaven or religion, a copy of it existed in the Annex. There were also all the documents written by the gods themselves about their own religions, and, in a way back section that you could only get into if Gavya was told to let you back there by the Speaker, were all the documents the Joint Commission wrote. I heard rumors that there was a complete history of Taikarlu and the Heka in there. That, I really wanted to read, but the Speaker had apparently decided I didn't need access to the restricted section for my job.

Gavya was at her station, like always. I decided that she would probably be the best person to ask my questions. I walked over to the desk and said hello.

Gavya turned to me. She was a beautiful woman, immortal and probably as old as the earth itself, but she looked to be in her early twenties. With light caramel skin, jet black eyes, long black hair down to her waist that she always wore down but never seemed to get in her way, she had an air of gracefulness. She was slender with long fingers, each one with a small but beautiful ring on it. She also had a small nose piercing in her right nostril and a Bindi, the small red dot on her forehead Hindu women sometimes adorn themselves with. Gavya was wearing a saree, like she normally did. Today, it was a vibrant green pattern with a gold trim.

"Bella," she greeted me, her voice light and soft, "you've come to study more?"

I smiled at her, "Of course. But first, can I talk to you for a bit?"

Gavya cocked her head to one side. Normally, I would only ask her to help me find the documents for one religion or another and she would just point me to the section containing that and we wouldn't talk again until I left. That's all anyone would really talk to Gavya about. So, it was probably a little weird for someone to actually want to have a conversation with her.

"Of course, Bella," she finally answered. "What do you wish to talk about?"

I paused for a moment. All those reasons it had been hard to make friends here came roaring back to me. After I was released from prison, a lot of people avoided me. I had made the gods mad with what I had done in the Trials Arena. Some of the other coordinators thought that I shouldn't have been allowed to stay in Taikarlu. As an unauthorized child, they thought I should have been destroyed, or at least just made only human. Others would be passingly nice to me, but feared losing their friends or angering the gods by hanging out with me.

A few, though, at least tried to be kind. Bob, for one, and Jim at the office. A few others too. But, soon, many of them distanced themselves from me. I am not sure if it was my questions about the Wastes that did it, or something else, but slowly anyone who had been friendly towards me backed off. Bob still would chat in passing and Jim had to talk to me for work. But others, Lydia and Jamison, Brandon and that one guy whose name I didn't know that lived on the third floor of my building who would talk with me in the hallway, eventually stopped talking. Now, when they see me, they will purposely become very busy or walk the other way. I would hate for Gavya to become like that too.

Gavya was watching me as I contemplated actually trying to discuss my curiosities with her. She waited patiently at first, but then apparently made the choice to speak first.

"You are afraid to speak, aren't you?" She asked gently. "No one has talked to you in a long time, and those that did before won't now, am I right?"

"Yeah," I sighed. "I don't know why."

Gavya furrowed her brow for a moment, then walked away. Not sure why, I just waited. Soon though, she returned with a small rolled-up paper in her hand. It had a bright red stamp on the outside of it.

Gavya handed me the paper and I examined the stamp. It was the seal of the First Joint Commission. This paper was from the off-limits area. Gavya should not have been showing this to me.

I unrolled the paper and read it. "Charter of Control, Edict 129: To prevent the return of chaos, there shall be no further mating with the human population unless prior approval is given by the Commission. Children of such matings shall be Warded. The Ward shall remain in such child until the time they die. Children made before this edict shall be subject to Warding if they display a lack of control of Heka or a willful disobedience under the Charter of Control. Pleasurable association with the Warded is just cause for reasonable suspicion of willful disobedience." There was more written on the paper, but it went on in a manner that made even less sense to me than that first paragraph did, so I stopped reading it.

"I know about that first bit, Gavya." I said. "That's why my father and I were arrested in the first place after my Trials Arena."

Gavya nodded. "Yes, you were a child who was not given prior approval to be born. But you could not control being born."

I reread the paper. "So, what's this about being Warded?"

"Your arm." Gavya gestured to my scar. "The thing they put inside you is a Ward. It keeps your Heka locked away from you, and your spirit contained to Taikarlu."

"But I can use some Heka," I said, confused.

Gavya thought for a moment, her eyebrows furrowed. "Maybe they have updated the Wards since their last use all those years ago. Maybe they made it so some Heka can be used. Gods and coordinators, and the dead, are here in spirit form only, Heka form. When children of gods or coordinators used to come here, to become one of us, they came in spirit form and would leave their human bodies behind, either dead or just vanished. The Wards were used to prevent out-of-control children's spirits from using Heka. The Commission made the Wards to block the Heka from them and protect everyone. But those out-of-control children weren't used as gods or coordinators, and you are. Maybe they made some adaptations for you."

Some of this made sense. "Is that why no one here glows?" I asked. I remembered when my father tested me to see if I had any Heka power before he brought me to attempt the Trials Arena. He had glowed like a glowstick. Then I had glowed in response. When he was teaching me how to use the Heka, he had me try to glow but only a little to show me how to keep It in check. But both those things had happened outside Taikarlu and the heavenly realms. Once inside, even when Dad or I was using our Heka, I didn't see anyone glow.

Gavya looked down at the floor, puzzled, "Glows? Oh, yes. That's right. To humans, when the Heka force is being used outside of Taikarlu, it appears as a glow." She turned to face me again. "The reason no one seems to glow here is that it is all spirit form. In spirit form, everything is the Heka force. Nothing seems to glow because literally everything is glowing."

"But the Trials Arena isn't in Taikarlu." I was now the one puzzled. "It's in Area One."

Gavya smiled softly. "It always amazes me how much we just understand intuitively here. And how much you without that intuition wouldn't know." She sighed. "Area One is part of Taikarlu. Everything here is part of Taikarlu, the jail you were held in, the city, all of the gods' heavens, hells, purgatories, all of it. Or at least used to be. You don't know about the Time of Chaos, the War, and the Separation."

I started pacing. There was so much going on in what Gavya was saying, I didn't know where to start asking questions. "Wait, so there was a war? Here? What is the Time of Chaos? And I still don't know how this piece of paper," I held up the roll I was still holding, "translates to no one wanting to talk to me. Or why you are right now when no one else will, for that matter."

Gavya sat down in her chair quietly. She closed her eyes, and was very still for so long, I wondered if I should just leave. But then she spoke, even softer than she had before, "I am talking to you because I don't care anymore. You are Warded. Based on the edict you hold in your hand, that means you either are dangerous because you cannot control your Heka, or because you are insane and choose not to control it. It means you can't be trusted. Many people here forgot that because it has been millennia since a Ward was used. They forgot that associating with a Warded meant that people would be suspicious of you, think that you would lose control too. Those who did talk to you at first must have been reminded by someone of that fact."

I felt myself getting angry, on top of being confused. "But I'm not dangerous!" I yelled. My pacing became more stomping. I walked around the circle desk over and over as I fumed. "I broke a rule I didn't know was a rule because no one taught me anything before I came here. So, they punish me for not knowing the rules by blocking my only way to know the rules? That's stupid! And even stupider to then turn around and block me from having any friends who could help me learn. What am I supposed to do, then? I already spent a hundred years just trying to learn the crap I need to know for that stupid job they make me do, and they won't let me in the restricted area, I'll bet--"

Gavya cut off my tirade, "You're right."

I stopped midstride. "I am?"

Gavya stood, came around to my side of the desk and put her hands on each of my shoulders, "Yes. They will not let you in the restricted area. They do not want you to learn for some reason. They don't want you to learn anything. I asked. Since you have been coming here, every day I have asked the Commission for permission to give you lessons on the history of Taikarlu, about everything. They keep telling me you don't need it. But you do, and I say as much to them. They blocked the Heka that allows you to just know all of this like the rest of us. Even humans who have passed on receive that much when they get to come to Taikarlu, whether they are rewarded or punished. But they keep insisting you will not need to be taught the knowledge."

As I listened to Gavya talk, my mouth hung open in surprise. She had been fighting to be allowed to teach me? I had a friend, a defender and didn't even know it. More importantly though, the gods were saying no. Why were they saying no? If I am to live in Taikarlu for eternity, I would need to know so many things about it. The only reason I wouldn't need to know all these things, how it worked, how the gods and coordinators really work, why they eat and go on vacation, was if my stay here was not permanent. But there was no way for me to leave, because of my punishment. Or was there?"

Gavya had still been talking while I was thinking. "Today, when you finally came to me, ready to seek the answers on your own, I decided I do not care. No one ever comes to the Annex anymore. So, who is to see me associate with a Warded? Even if they do, what do I care if they become suspicious of me? Ward me too? It won't matter. I hardly use my Heka anymore anyway since the invention of computers. Any human librarian anywhere could do my job now with ease. So, I will teach you. Permission or not. And I will help you too. Help you to find out why they don't want you learning about Taikarlu, about the Chaos and the War and whatever else it is they are trying to hide from you. Because believe me, there is something, and I will find out what. And why."

There was a time in my life when I didn't have many questions. A time when I just went to school, learned a bunch of stuff I didn't really care about and went home. Back then, I always wished for something more exciting in life. I really miss those days. Now, I have so many questions. So many no one seems to want to let me find the answer for. I have that excitement I wished for, but now I regret asking for it.

With so many questions in my mind, again, I didn't know what to say to Gavya. What do you say to someone who declares that they are going to risk being punished by all the gods that ever have or ever will exist to help you? Apparently, you ask them "Why do the gods need apartments?" because that is what I said.

Gavya laughed. She laughed really hard and long, so much so that she snorted. I didn't think someone a beautiful and graceful as her could snort. But she did. It seemed to catch her off-guard too because it made her stop laughing. Or at least, calm down to a chuckle.

"Apparently, we need to really start at the beginning of the beginning. Didn't your father teach you anything before bringing you to the Trials?"

I shrugged, "The gods of all the religions ever exist, there are coordinators who help out the gods, we have a power called the Heka and live in a pretty cool place. In really simple terms, that pretty much sums up what he told me."

"And you passed the Trials Arena on just that?" Gavya sounded amazed. "Come here, dear. I think we will take a walk, grab some snacks and coffee, then you and I will discuss everything."

Bella Part Two

I sat back in my chair and sipped my coffee. It had long since gone cold. This was day three of going to the Annex and not doing any research. That first day, Gavya and I had talked for what seemed like hours. Eventually, I made myself go home. I had been hiding the fact that I was nodding off while she talked. After I slept, I woke on what I considered the next day, went to work for a while and when Dad came to relieve me, I didn't even bother changing before heading straight to the Annex to talk more. Gavya had guessed that would be my plan and had already grabbed food and drinks for us, well really me. Again, I only left when I could barely keep my eyes open. Today, when I woke up, I packed some clothes to change into at the Annex and had gone to work.

Upon arriving at the Annex, I changed and ate while Gavya kept talking. It was late again. But I refused to fall asleep this time until I wanted to. So, I chugged cold coffee and thought over everything she had taught me.

A long time ago, apparently, the Heka was not just a force. It was real, as real as the gods. It was over the gods. It had a body. Back then, there was no Joint Commission, no Speaker who led the Joint Commission, nothing. Taikarlu was all one place, all linked together. The Heka created the gods, coordinators, humans, everything, using Its own power. It imbued Its power into everything It created at the level each thing would need for what its role was. Gods got a lot, coordinators some, humans less, and animals and plants just a dab. Places had more or less, depending on whether it was in Taikarlu or in the human realms.

The gods were not equal though. Their level of power, of Heka, was based on the number of worshippers they had. Since this was way at the beginning of human existence, some religions weren't even founded yet and had no worshippers. The gods of those religions didn't get much say, or much time with Heka. Some of them tried to force themselves to be recognized before their time by coming to the human realms and having children. Sometimes, coordinators thought that they could improve their lot in life by getting worshipped as gods, and copied the gods' idea.

The more gods and coordinators that did this, the less and less they listened to the Heka. Gavya called this the Time of Chaos. To try to fix this, to try to get the gods working together again, the Heka created the Joint Commission. But It made a fatal flaw. It didn't change the power structure. Gods with lots of worshippers used the Heka power inside themselves to take higher positions by force from the gods with few or no worshippers. To gain more Heka power and be able to bully their way into better positions, some gods decided to try to convince their worshippers that they were the only right religion and that to have anything good after death, they needed to convince others to sign up. They thought that more gods within one religion meant more choices for the humans to worship, which would mean more humans would choose their faith over another. Gods for some religions started having lots and lots of children, making many demigods, and getting their coordinators to have lots of children so they would have more workers in the human realms to preach their message. This pushing of one religion over another by so many different faiths caused even more problems because we know how humans are.

These battles for power in the gods led to battles of being the only one right in the humans. It led to wars, forced conversions and lots of violence. As worshippers were stolen from one religion and forced to another, or murdered because they refused, the gods in Taikarlu got angry with each other and started to fight one another.

Gods started erecting barricades to prevent the people from different religions from coming to their heaven. Taikarlu got split up.

This is where Gavya's story got complicated. Not understanding all of how the Heka works, or how it worked when It was a walking, talking person, the idea of the gods overpowering their creator seems strange to me. But according to Gavya, that is just what was happening. The Heka was not just standing idly by as all this was happening, but was trying to fix the issues between the gods. Gavya said the Heka had always intended for the gods and coordinators to work together, be one whole with lots of different parts, and never thought that one part would become jealous of another. The Heka apparently tried to listen to all the gods at the newly formed Joint Commission, as its head, but some gods did not want the Heka to be the head of the Joint Commission anymore. Some wanted the Heka to still be the head but for the power of the positions within the Commission to be more evenly distributed. Many gods had many ideas of how to make the system fairer, or better in their eyes.

While the Heka tried to listen to all of Its creations to make things better for everyone, the rules It had made were ignored by many gods who were intent to just grab as much power as they could. The more It tried to push back to regain control of Taikarlu, the more these gods got angry and wanted to be given a better position, or wanted to protect the position they had. There were some gods that were fighting on the side of the Heka, for Its right as our creator to assign laws and rules and positions to everyone. The fighting between the gods and coordinators in Taikarlu, and the fighting between the humans in their realm just got worse and worse.

At this point Gavya pulled out a map of Taikarlu. She pointed to all the places on the map I knew. Area One, Central Hub which I now knew meant all of the areas of the city rather than just my part of it, and the areas controlled by religions I already learned about and the places their worshippers could go after death, she showed me on the map. Then she showed me and named the places for faiths I hadn't learned about yet. Finally, Gavya pointed to an area of the map I hadn't noticed before. It was off the western edge, surrounded by a wider expanse of the Wastelands than anywhere else. The actual lands for this place ran off the edge of the map in a way that looked intentional.

Gavya told me that this place used to be called Area Two. Area Two had been an area designated for the gods' leisure. No humans had ever been allowed there. No coordinators either, so Gavya, as a coordinator, was not sure what it had looked like before the War. But she had heard it was beautiful.

As the fighting amongst the gods wore on, eventually the different sides, those for returning all power to the Heka and those for taking control themselves, drew battle lines across Area Two. One day the two sides drew weapons and clashed. Since they were all gods, they were all immortal, so no one side could ever gain an advantage. They could injure each other, cause each other to bleed, but eventually the injured god would heal themselves and return to the fight. There were more gods on the side for taking power for themselves, but since they couldn't truly stop the gods who wanted the Heka to take full control again, the War ended up like rippling sands in the tide. The power would move from one side to another and back again without anyone ever being declared the winner.

The War lasted three days. In those three days, all the gods ignored the humans they were bound to. The gods fighting were too embroiled to remember their duties. The gods not involved were either fleeing or pleading with the Heka to do something. The coordinators were at a loss, torn between assisting their gods in Area Two, where they were not allowed, or tending the neglected human realm the best they could. In the end, things in the human realm broke down. Three days in Taikarlu of no godly action meant years of absence for the humans. Unending winters, famine, natural disasters and fighting ensued. Times were dark for the humans and much of the progress the humans made, learning and evolving, technological advances and written languages were all lost.

On the third day, a handful of gods from both sides left the battle. Gavya told me that to this day, they are not sure where those gods went. They were never seen again. But when they left, something changed. No one is quite sure what happened. Most people assume that the Heka just broke down and gave up. Some believe the Heka decided to punish the gods. Some think that the gods who left the War at Area Two did something. All they did know is that one day Taikarlu was beautiful and, even with the fighting between the gods, every god could go to the humans, be seen, conduct miracles, whatever. Even with limited power from the Heka, they could still do all this. Everything was the way they had always known.

Everyone in Taikarlu heard the first peal of thunder. That they know for sure. Not just in Taikarlu, but everyone did. The humans on earth did too. Then came the rain. It rained hard for days, causing flooding. Rushing water covered the earth and covered Taikarlu. Eventually, the waves were so tall were that the sun was blocked out. Gods drowned. Coordinators drowned. People, animals, everything drowned. The world, both the earth and Taikarlu went silent.

Drowned but alive, the gods and coordinators could hear the silence but their Heka was muted. They could not feel the connection to that power as they floated in dark, cold water, seeing no one else. Time passed, how much no one knows. With no light, no sound, no one else around, each god and coordinator was an island alone with no way to guess if it had been hours, days or years. Some were terrified this was the way they would stay for eternity.

But it didn't. Eventually, the waters receded and everything was changed. Their Heka power was back at full strength. Actually, It was better than full strength. It was equal for all the gods and coordinators. But It was limited. Coordinators could only use the Heka within the scope of their jobs. Gods could only use It on their worshippers and in their lands. Miracles and special acts were hard, and couldn't be done in ways humans could visibly see anymore. No towers of fire or bushes that can speak.

Taikarlu was changed too. The walls the gods had erected between their lands had all tumbled down. Where the walls landed, the ground had broken apart. Miles and miles of wasteland, dry, empty desert now stood between one heaven and another, between one hell, purgatory, godly area, coordinator platform, and another. The dry, empty Wastes made travel between each land impossible on foot. Many gods and coordinators had tried in the beginning to traverse the Wastes between their lands and another. Each time, they ended up back where they had started from. Sometimes within minutes, sometimes years later, trying to cross the sands of the Wastes always led to walking in a full circle. Using technology like compasses didn't help either. Maps were created with the assumption that the land in Taikarlu had just spread out, but each area had retained its relative position in relation to each other, but no one knew for sure if this was true. The inhabitants of Taikarlu called this the Separation. Though technology designed by the gods allowed easier travel between parts of Taikarlu and the human realm now, there were still boundaries on what could be done, and where one could go.

Most importantly, the Heka was gone. The embodiment of the Heka had vanished. No one could speak to It anymore, not directly, not the way they had before. Gavya assumed no one knew where the Heka vanished to, because if anyone did know where the Heka was, they were not saying. The power was still around, so It must be still alive somewhere, but no one knew how or where. The Separation took so much with it. Before the Separation, there had been so many fantastic beasts, what humans know as mythical animals. Dragons and unicorns, djinns and golems, fairies and leprechauns, all existed in Taikarlu. But when the Heka vanished, they vanished too.

This woke the gods up to see their foolishness for what is really was. The Joint Commission came together and set down new rules to stop the Chaos from ever happening again. Children were outlawed, religions were given freedom over their own worshippers and were told to not interfere with others. But the damage was done for the humans. They had been told once that they should fight for their faith to be the best and only. The gods no longer had the power to walk amongst them like before, so they had no way to tell their worshippers to stop. For the humans, the wars and fighting, proselytizing and killing continued. The gods and coordinators did the best they could to stem the tide, but there is not much they can do unless the Heka returns and changes things again.

Gavya told me all of this with maps and papers, books and written first-hand accounts. She even told me about her days drowned. She shuddered as she spoke about that, the fear from that time still very real to her. As I sipped my coffee and listened to her talk for three days, I hadn't wanted to interrupt with questions. By just listening, and letting her tell the story her way, Gavya eventually answered all my questions without me asking them anyway. All of them except one.

"So," Gavya finally said, "you are pretty much caught up. For the last couple or so thousand years in human time, that has been how we all lived. Adhere to the Commission rules and wait to see if the Heka returns. Then your dad decided he wanted a kid. And he took that kid through the Trials and that kid claims to have spoken to the Heka. Not with a sense of the Heka, but the actual Heka, with words. Now many fear the Chaos will return. The Joint Commission let you live and be a coordinator. Will others fall away from the hard-won peace too now? They are scared, and all they can do is stick to the Commission rules as hard as possible in hopes they can keep the Chaos at bay."

Gavya sat back in her chair. She looked around the circle desk at the spread of documents. Most of them were from the restricted section. If anyone walked in on us now, we both would be in a world of trouble. Gavya sighed and stretched, moving as if she would begin to clean up.

"But there's one thing that doesn't make any sense in all of that." I said.

Gavya stopped. "What doesn't make sense?"

"Why did the Heka allow any of it to happen?" I asked her.

Gavya looked at me, hard, almost like the question made her angry. "What do you mean allow it? The Heka didn't allow the Chaos, the gods made it happen."

Thinking she didn't understand what I meant, I rethought my question for a moment before speaking. "The Heka, the embodied Heka, It's basically the god of the gods, right?"

Gavya nodded. "That's one way to put it."

"So, why did the Heka let this happen?" I asked again. "If the Heka was the god of the gods, It was also the god of man and the coordinators, and everything. Why didn't It just not give any of them, any of us, free will? Why didn't It just take away free will when It realized us having it was messing things up?"

Gavya breathed deeply and then let that breath out slowly through pursed lips. She sat back down. "It's like this…" She started, then stopped. Taking another long breath, Gavya spoke again. "Ok, so consider your job as a coordinator. You make decisions in that job, right?"

I nodded. I made a lot of decisions in my job every day. Was that person's anger bad enough to be considered immoral by their religion's rules? Should I apply an Eastern interpretation or a Western interpretation of that text for the person who lived in the border between the two? Was that person at sixteen years old wise enough to understand right from wrong in that particular instance where they hit someone, or was their prefrontal cortex too underdeveloped at that moment to really understand and that should be considered a childhood crime?

Gavya saw in my face that I understood what she meant. "To make decisions means to make a choice. You have to choose yes or no, choose left or right. Choice can't happen if there is no free will, because choice is free will and free will means choice. You with me so far?"

You have to have free will to make choices, makes sense. I nodded to show I was following.

"The Heka made the choice to make everything, meaning the Heka has free will." Gavya stood, stretching again as she talked. "It made the choice to make everything from Itself, from Heka, to give Heka to every living thing. Everything's spirit, whether it has a physical body or not, has some Heka in it. Which means some of that free will that is in the Heka had to be given to each thing. Just as you can't take parts of yourself away and still be the same, the Heka couldn't either. When It chose to make us all out of bits of Itself, It had to include the free will bit in there. The more Heka something has, the more free will it has."

"So," I said slowly, thinking as I talked, "if the Heka had chosen to make people, the gods, whatever, out of something else, It wouldn't have had to let us have free will? But because It chose to use Itself to make us, It had to give free will to us?"

Gavya nodded. "Pretty much, except for one thing. When the

35

Heka created everything, there was nothing but Itself. All that existed was Heka, was power. Remember, the Heka isn't a person, not even kind of a person like the gods and coordinators. The Heka is just power. For a time, the Heka made Itself seem corporeal, seem like It had a body, but that was just a way for It to move around inside Its creation. In reality, the Heka has no form. It is just raw power."

Gavya stopped for a moment and thought. When she spoke again, she seemed unsure of what she was saying. "I guess the Heka could have created something before creating all of this and then created us all from that thing. But again, where would that thing be created from? From the Heka, which means the power of the Heka. So, that thing would have free will, and would have given it to us anyway."

Gavya stopped again, then said, surer this time. "Yes, definitely. Because the Heka is power, and that power contains the ability to make choices, anything the Heka created would have to have the power to make choices. And anything created from that would have the power to make choices too. Free will was inevitable, not a choice the Heka made. And if the Heka didn't make the choice to give us free will, It didn't have the power to take it away."

I thought about that for a time. "So, the Heka didn't have the free will to give or not give us free will. We just had it because It had it."

Gavya nodded. "Exactly."

"Is that why coordinators take time off? Or gods want to eat even though they don't need to?" I asked, finally getting back to the question that had started all this three days ago.

"Yes." Gavya responded. "The power of choice means having free will. Free will means having desires. You have to desire what you are choosing. That means that gods, coordinators, humans, animals, we all have desires. Needs are what the physical form drives us to desire. Since gods and coordinators don't have real physical forms, bodies like humans and animals, they don't have needs. But they still have desires, they still have wants, because they have free will. Those in Taikarlu just have enough access to the Heka power to obtain their desires instantly, or almost instantly. The humans allowed here benefit from the access the gods have created, or in the case of those being punished, feel the lack because their access is blocked. Humans on earth have to struggle to get their wants, and needs, because they don't have as much access to Heka."

Suddenly, a lot of things made sense to me. "Gavya, can I tell you something I have never told anyone else?"

Gavya was surprised by my sudden change in topic. "Of course."

I held out my right arm to her, showing my scar from the implant, the Ward. "It hurts." I told Gavya. "Sometimes it hurts. Pain will move through my arm, shooting up and down the implant. I mean, the Ward. I was told I shouldn't even know it was there but sometimes it hurts."

Gavya's eyes got really wide. Her mouth dropped open. "That shouldn't... that isn't possible. Wards don't hurt. They never hurt."

"Mine does," I told her firmly, "and I think I know why."

Gavya still stared at me. She closed her mouth, but I think it took an act of will on her part to do it.

When she didn't speak, I continued. "I'm human, Gavya. Wards are meant for spirits that don't have needs. If the Heka power is free will, and free will is choices and desire, then limiting someone's Heka limits their wants. I don't just have wants. I'm human, I have needs too. Needs are choices that don't come from free will. I need to eat, that is not free will. I can make the choice to go hungry, but then I die. I can choose to eat later, but then my stomach hurts, or I get dizzy from low blood sugar. I can choose to eat this rather than that, and that is free will, but I don't truly have the free will to choose not to eat."

Gavya started to speak. She opened her mouth and made a sound, but then quickly closed it again. The expression on her face seemed like she wanted to contradict me but then decided against it.

When she didn't try to talk again, I continued. "The same goes with sleep, and other stuff. That's why the Housing had to build me a bathroom, and bedroom. Because I am still human and have needs. Needs that make me make a choice. But the Ward wants to block my choices by blocking my Heka. So, when I need something, when my human body is hungry, the Ward hurts me. It is trying to block a want that isn't a want."

Gavya and I sat in silence for what felt like a long time after I finished speaking. She continued to stare at me, her face showing every emotion she felt. Surprise, then wonder, disbelief then anger. I could tell the moment she became resolute.

"No." Gavya whispered. She said it so softly, I could barely hear her.

"What?" I asked.

"No." she said again, only slightly louder. "It doesn't work like that. You don't have needs. You can't. I don't know why your Ward hurts sometimes, but it isn't because you have needs."

Now, it was my turn to stare in disbelief at Gavya. "Yes, I do." I told her. "I have needs. I have always had needs. I am human, remember? Humans have physical bodies that have needs, like food. They never made me not human, so I still have needs."

"That's not the way it works!" Gavya said firmly. "Who told you that you were still human?"

My mouth dropped open, and I know my face went through all the emotions I just saw Gavya's go through. But I was able to speak again faster than she was. "Who told me I was still human? No one. No one needed to. I am human, in a human body. I never left my body to come here to do the Trials Arena. Remember, that's the one thing they found me absolutely guilty of, being a human in the Trials Arena."

Gavya tried to interrupt at this point. She seemed like she still wanted to disagree with me but I stopped her. "Gavya," I tried to speak more calmly, "after spending seventeen years in a human body that gets hungry and tired and has to pee, don't you think I would know if I am not in that body anymore? Don't you think I would notice not needing food anymore? I get hungry, Gavya. Not just wanting food because it tastes good but really needing it. Hell, three days ago I passed out in my apartment because I forgot to eat for too long. Haven't you seen me here while you were telling me the history of Taikarlu getting sleepy and nodding off in my chair? Why would I do that if I didn't need sleep?"

Gavya didn't answer me. Again, her face went through

contortions that said she was warring with different feelings and ways to respond. Then, with no warning, Gavya got up and walked away.

When she returned, Gavya was carrying a heavy looking book. The book was about as long as my arm and as probably a foot wide. It was so thick that Gavya's long delicate fingers could not wrap around the spine from front cover to back cover to hold it. Instead, she cradled it in her arms like a baby. Setting it down in front of me, Gavya opened the cover and began flipping through the pages. Even that thick, the pages were still thin like onion skin. There must have been a million pages or more in that book. Gavya turned the pages in bunches, stopping to scan this page and that. Finally, she closed the book and walked away again.

While I waited for her to return, I examined the cover of the huge book. It was leather, a strange looking, thick leather. I reached out to touch it, wondering if that weird leather felt as scaley as it looked, but for some reason, my brain just recoiled at the idea of touching the book. There were letters, or symbols of some type, burned into the leather cover.

Gavya returned, and at first, I thought she came back empty handed. But then I saw in her left hand the tiniest book I had ever seen. Smaller than the palm of her hand, I was sure that when she opened it, we would need a magnifying glass to read it. She sat down at the circle desk, on the opposite side than me and made a space for the book on the counter.

Gavya opened the book and the words jumped off the page, like literally. Hovering in the air were words in sentences and paragraphs, like glowing bits of light. Gavya scanned the hovering words, then looked down at the book to turn a few pages. She read again, then turned the book towards me. The words in the air flipped so they were facing me right ways.

"Read this." Gavya told me.

I read the page. "The amount of Heka contained within Taikarlu exceeds the capacity of the human physical body to withstand for long. After numerous scientific evaluations, Stenadium the Physician has determined that the human body can only withstand Heka levels of 8.2... what is that word?"

"Zynoteis," Gavya told me. "It's a measurement of how strong Heka is. Your report from the Trials Arena would have measured your Heka levels and reported It in Zynoteis."

"Oh, I never saw my Trials Arena report," I told her, then continued reading, "8.2 Zynoteis. At a level of over 13 Zynoteis, Taikarlu is too strong for the human frame to maintain residence for long. Anything over twelve earthly hours will cause the human body discomfort. At twenty-four earthly hours, the human organs will begin to decay. After two full earthly days, the human will expire from Heka poisoning. In any situation requiring humans to remain in Taikarlu, such as oracle transmittance, it is suggested the human be advised to relinquish their body on earth. Otherwise, the pain of the Heka poisoning will overpower their being and potentially rupture their spirit beyond viability."

Gavya looked at me, kindly. "Do you understand what that just said? It says they tested this stuff. You are not here in a human body. You never could have been. You would have been poisoned by the Heka and your human body would have died so painfully it would have destroyed your spirit."

I thought about this for a long while before I responded. How could I have come here without my human body and not have known I left it behind? Then I remembered. When I told Dad that I agreed to come to do the Trials Arena and work with him after, he had given me that foul tasting tea. It made me go to sleep very fast, then just wake up like nothing ever happened. I had woken up feeling the greatest I had ever felt. Was that because I didn't actually wake up, but my spirit had left my body? No, Dad would have told me. Wouldn't he?

Dad had been rushing me around so much that day, so fast. He wouldn't have even explained how to use Heka to me before throwing me into the Trials Arena if I hadn't had basically pitched a teenage fit in the street. Plus, Dad obviously was not telling me a lot of things that he should have back then. Like that my very existence was completely illegal and he and I were both risking a punishment of death by having me do the Trials Arena. Like that he lied to get access to Area One in the first place. Like that you shouldn't mess with time.

Yeah, Dad forgot to tell me a lot of important things. So, why was it hard to accept that maybe he forgot to tell me that my physical human body had been on earth this whole time and I was just a spirit?

It wasn't. It wasn't and that was a whole new reason for me to be angry with him. He never told me that I was leaving my body behind. If that is what actually happened. But if it did, that still left me with questions. "So, why do I still get hungry and tired and whatever?"

Gavya thought about this for a moment. "Is it possible you don't? You just think you do? You have thought you were still human so you convinced yourself that your wants were actually still needs?"

I rolled that idea around in my head for a moment but it didn't work. "Nah, if that were the case, why did the Commission have Housing add a bedroom and bathroom to my apartment? If I don't actually need to pee, why would they let me keep thinking I do? Wouldn't they have told me the truth?"

"Why would they say you don't need to learn the history of Taikarlu? Why would they do anything they do?" Gavya didn't try to hide her frustration with them as she spoke. "I couldn't guess at their reasons for letting you believe, and act, like you are still in a human body, but there is an easy way to test this. Stay here. Don't leave."

"Huh?" I asked. "Where are you going?"

Gavya smiled. "No, I mean don't go back to your apartment. Let's test your needs over wants. Humans will need water within three earthly days. To show you your needs are not really needs, stay here. Don't eat or drink anything for three days. When you don't actually become dehydrated, or only feel like you are but actually are fine, you will know the truth."

"Alright." I agreed. Maybe I was just confused. Maybe not knowing I didn't have a physical body had made me think I needed this stuff when I didn't. Maybe I had assumed way too much without really understanding anything. (And whose fault would that be? The Commission's of course. They, like Dad, kept me in the dark about way too much apparently.) Or maybe, Gavya was wrong. "But if I say it's a need, I need the water, I am dehydrated, you need to believe me."

Gavya stepped over to her computer, typed something, and then looked back at me. "Symptoms of dehydration include dry mouth, fever, headache, confusion, and dizziness along with some other stuff. If you experience any of that, and it doesn't go away, then you are dehydrated. But I really don't believe you will."

So, we put it to the test. Gavya pulled out an earthly based clock from somewhere to keep track of real time, and I went to work on all the studying of religions I should have been doing those past few days. I didn't worry about work. Dad could just deal with it. All I worried about for the next sixteen hours, according to the non-Taikarlu clock, was how Indigenous Americans tribes in the United States differed on beliefs about the afterlife.

I only say sixteen hours because that's how long it took to prove Gavya wrong. As much as I had tried to ignore it, by hour sixteen my mouth felt like sandpaper and my head was pounding. The words on the pages of the book I was reading seemed to swim in and out of focus. The feeling started about hour ten, and I took a nap. When I woke up four hours later, my discomfort was worse.

Gavya came to where I had made myself a nest in the aisle between one bookshelf containing United States' Indigenous American beliefs and another containing books on Canadian First Nations beliefs. "So, in further research on dehydration, apparently an over-consumption of caffeine can speed up the process, so I thought I would come check on… Woah, you don't look good."

"Yeah, thanks for that." I tried to say, but apparently my tongue was not cooperating.

Gavya knelt down and put her hand on my forehead. It felt very cooling. She tsked. "Your skin is very dry and your head is warm. Do you have a headache, feel bad in any way?"

I nodded yes, since my mouth didn't work.

Gavya rocked back on her heels, thinking, "Huh. You must actually be getting dehydrated. That means water would be a need for you. But how?" She sat there, staring into space, still thinking to herself.

I poked her, and she looked at me again. "Oh crap!" She exclaimed. "Yeah, water. I'll get you water."

Gavya came back with several bottles of water and over the next few hours, she forced me to drink little sips. In between sips, I laid on the floor and slept. But only for what felt like a few moments, and then Gavya was waking me again to take a few more sips. After three bottles and what felt like forever, I woke up feeling much better. Tired, for sure, and still a little bit of a headache, but my mouth didn't feel like sandpaper anymore.

I sat up and drank more than a few sips. "Got anything to eat?" I asked. "I'm starving."

Gavya ran away and came back with a peanut butter sandwich and some plain potato chips. As I ate, we talked.

"So, not human huh?" I asked sarcastically.

"No, not human," Gavya replied, "but something. Something not right. How's your arm?"

I looked down at my scar and realized it was hurting worse than it ever had. "Hurts like a bitch," I told her.

"I think maybe you were right." Gavya was staring off thoughtfully. "The Ward malfunctions because you have needs you shouldn't have. The question is why do you have needs?"

I looked at Gavya. The answer was obvious to me. "Because you were wrong. Because that Stenadium guy was wrong. Because I am still in my human body. Even here in Taikarlu, somehow my human body is surviving all this Heka power. Hell, in the court trial, when they were talking about my Trials Arena results, Jim told me I passed at a level that could have made me a top-tier god. Maybe I have way more Heka than a child of a human and a coordinator should for some reason and that makes my human body able to withstand the Heka in Taikarlu better than a human body should."

Gavya thought about this for a bit. Then she slowly said, "Or maybe because you are not in your human body." When I began to protest, she put her hand up to stop me. "I am not saying you don't have a human body. We just proved you have human needs so obviously you have a human body. I am just saying, you are not in your human body."

I shook my head, disagreeing. "That's not possible." I pulled over one of the books I had been reading while still lucid. I showed her the book, and pointed out what I had read. "I know that humans get stuff wrong sometimes, but a lot of the Indigenous Peoples in a lot of places say the same thing about this, so they probably have it at least mostly right. According to these documents, leaving a spirit separated from its body too long will result in the body becoming ill or even dying. My spirit can't have been outside my body for a hundred years and my body not have died yet. Even if time is different in the earthly places, I am sure a hundred spirit years is too long in earthly time. Plus, it also says that when my body sleeps, my spirit would search for my body and rejoin it. I haven't done that."

Gavya thought, reading the page I had shown her. "But your spirit wouldn't have been able to search for your body. The Ward locked it in Taikarlu." She paused, reading the page some more. "If your spirit is away from your body too long, the body dies, but that still leaves your spirit here, free." Gavya stood and rummaged on a shelf, pulled out a few different books, opened one up and showed it to me. It was from another faith, which one I wasn't sure. "Except, according to this, because the body and spirit weren't linked at the death, the soul didn't transfer too. This leaves the spirit lost and confused, slowly forgetting who it was, not knowing where it is or where it is going. The spirit will wither and fall, wandering around in a void until it disappears."

I looked down at my arm. The scar was bright pink against my pale, sickly skin. This long, thin snake running from my elbow to my wrist. What was under there? What was the Ward truly? What had the Joint Commission done to me?

"When I passed out in my bedroom," I told Gavya, "I thought I heard my old teacher from before. It felt like she was talking to me, trying to wake me up. I assumed it was just my mind playing tricks on me, because I hadn't eaten in too long. But what if it wasn't? What if the Commission put the Ward in me to keep my body and my spirit separate, and when I passed out, I made some sort of link with myself?"

Gavya's anger would have been clear to anyone with half an eye. "If they did that, if the Commission separated your spirit and your body, they did it knowing it would kill you. That's why they said you wouldn't need the knowledge. Because they assumed you would die soon."

I didn't respond. The idea that they did that. That would be murder. At least in my mind it would be. Gavya spoke again. "That would mean they violated their oaths. They made an oath under the Heka to punish you for your crimes the way the humans decided, either as a human or as a coordinator for eternity. Making you both and to die as both wasn't one of the choices they had."

"What would that mean, if they violated their oaths?" I asked.

"Death. The Heka ruled a long time ago, when It first tried to make a Commission, that any oaths the Commission made, it must stick to. Violate that oath and the Heka would remove Itself from you. Without any Heka at all, a god can't have any worshippers. Without the Heka, a god withers away, sort of in the same way this book said a spirit would if the body died because it never returned. It would be a painful, horrifying experience for any full god to have. And the end result would be that god disappearing from existence, the closest thing to dying a god could ever get."

"But the Heka vanished, the manifestation vanished." I rubbed my forehead. This was sounding more and more like someone had planned this, planned to harm me, no matter what the outcome of my trial was, and the idea of that scared me. The idea that the gods thought they could do that scared me. "Why would the gods care what the punishment was a long time ago if the Heka isn't here to enact it?"

"Maybe some gods thought they could get away with violating their oaths because the corporeal Heka has been gone for so long." Gavya sighed, sitting back. "The Heka hasn't been around to control things for a long time and the Joint Commission has overturned some old rules and made some new ones. Maybe they think that rule made by the Heka isn't enforceable anymore and they could get rid of a problem child with too much power by just letting her die, spirit disconnected from the body. Body dies, spirit withers away, lost, confused and no longer powerful."

Bella Part Three

Gavya and I had been alone in the Annex for days. Not just days in earthly time, but days in Taikarlu time as well. I had not gone to work or to my apartment. We had spent this time researching anything we could that might lead us to some sort of answer to how the Commission would have separated my body from my spirit and how to prove that they actually were separated, well more proof than a simple dehydration test showing I had human needs. And why. We also looked for what we could do about it.

The entire time, my arm where the Ward was implanted hurt. Not the sudden, jolting pain I got occasionally, but a full time, low-key throbbing that I mostly ignored. I convinced myself that the throbbing had always been there, just beneath the surface and I hadn't noticed it because I wasn't thinking about it. In reality, I knew it was a warning about something.

Gavya and I were in the restricted section, reviewing scrolls that she thought might contain helpful information, when there was a loud bang from the main room of the Annex. Someone else was there.

Hidden behind stacks of scrolls and books, in the cage that locked the restricted section, I couldn't see who it was. But I knew anyway. There was a tightening in the muscles of my legs and arms. I could still move, but it was difficult. A flash of pain, like razors, went through my right arm, and I bit my lip to keep from crying out. The newcomer to the Annex were Avenging Women and they were here for me.

The Avenging Women were women who looked a lot like how humans describe angels. Their skin and eyes were the color of skim milk. Their hair, also white, flowed down their back to lay between their six white wings and stop at their knees. The Women were warriors, who wore white armor. I had first encountered them when the Avenging Women had arrested my father and I after I completed the Trials Arena. With a look, the Women can render the person in their gaze powerless to move. They can also hear thoughts. I learned when I was on trial for the crimes the Commission said I committed that they were basically the police of Taikarlu. My research on them had taught me that, concealed in their armor, each Avenging Woman kept a whip capable of at least harming gods, coordinators, and humans alike. If that whip could actually kill a god... well, no one had gotten close enough to try.

The Avenging Women were technically coordinators, but special ones. There had been no Avenging Women when the Heka walked around in a visible body. They had appeared after the Separation. The documents I had read were not sure if they had been created by the Heka before It vanished or if they had been created by some of the gods on the Commission. But they all agreed the Avenging Women's job was to uphold the law.

Laws that, apparently, I was breaking by no longer going to work. Since they couldn't see me, the Avenging Women's power to incapacitate was not in full force. Gavya saw my face fill with fear and peeked around the shelves hiding us.

"Shit," she whispered, "Avenging Women, six of them."

"Yeah," I whispered back, sarcastically, "tell me something my paralyzing fear doesn't already know."

Gavya looked at me and realized I was stiffening up the closer the Women got to the back of the Annex. She glanced around the shelves again. "They appear to be searching up and down each row of the Annex. So, they can't know exactly where you are in here. But they are definitely looking for you. I wonder why? They are getting closer."

"There is no way they are here to just make sure I'm doing ok, like a friendly welfare check. My arm feels like it is going to fall off!"

I said through gritted teeth. "Is there another exit to this place?"

Gavya thought for a moment, which seemed like an eternity. I could not only hear the Avenging Women getting closer, but feel it as my very muscles seemed to tighten and turn to stone, and my arm began to pound in time with my heart.

Suddenly, Gavya grabbed a bunch of the scrolls and books we had just been looking through and shoved them into the waistband of her saree. Then she handed me a handful of scrolls and gestured for me to hide them on my person somehow. As I stuffed them down my shirt, Gavya grabbed my free hand and led me further into the restricted section. She had to almost drag me because my legs were so tense that I could barely shuffle my feet along.

As we wound our way through the bowels of the restricted section, Gavya kept whispering. "This is not ok. This is not ok."

Finally, we reached the back wall of the Annex. It looked to me like a dead end, but Gavya reached out and started pulling on one scroll, then pushing it back in place, then pulling on another one. "Which one? Which one is it?" She mumbled. Finally, she pulled a thick scroll that was falling to pieces and, instead of the scroll sliding off the shelf, the whole bookshelf that it was sitting on tipped forward. None of the scrolls on the bookshelf fell.

Gavya reached behind the tipped bookshelf, feeling along the wall until we heard a click. Both of us turned to look behind us, afraid the Avenging Women would have heard the noise, but they hadn't reached the restricted section yet. Gavya pushed on whatever had made the click and then moved her arm. Once she did, the back wall of the Annex and the bookshelf connected to it opened up like a door to reveal a courtyard outside. We slid through the opening and stepped out into the courtyard, or well, Gavya stepped, I shuffled. Once we were safely outside, Gavya pushed the wall back closed and the bricks around the opening seamlessly fit back together with the actual wall, hiding that there had ever been any doorway there.

With the walls of the building between me and the Avenging Women, their grip on me slacked. My muscles still felt heavy, but I was able to move freely. The pain in my right arm, though, did not diminish. In fact, if anything, it got worse.

Gavya leaned against the building for a moment, breathing heavily. "I stole from the Annex. Holy crap, I stole from the Annex."

"Gavya." I said gently, trying not to interrupt her existential crisis, "I really can't stay here. The Avenging Women will eventually find me."

Gavya closed her eyes, sighed, then opened them again. "Ok Bella, but where do you go?"

"My apartment..." I started to say but Gavya shook her head.

It will be crawling with Avenging Women." She looked down at me. "By the way you are rubbing your arm, I would guess they are tracking you with the Ward, and that is making it hurt. And if they can't find you, the first place they would expect you to go is home."

I looked down and realized I had been rubbing my arm like she said. I stopped myself, and tried to think, "My dad..." I started again.

Again, Gavya shook her head no. "That would be the second place they would look. You need someplace the Avenging Women could never be sent to look for you. Someplace the gods would never think to look for you."

"The gods?" I asked. "What do the gods have to do with the Avenging Women? Aren't the Women just like a police force or something?"

Gavya nodded. "Basically. But just like the police for humans need a warrant to come arrest someone, so do the Avenging Women. They are tasked by the laws. At first, it was the laws the Heka made before It disappeared. Now, with the Heka gone and the Joint Commission in place making new laws, they are tasked with upholding the Joint Commission laws. To get them to act, to track and detain someone, one or more of the gods have to show that a Joint Commission law, or a contract made with the Joint Commission, has been violated. I guess the gods consider your failure to show up to work in a long time a violation of your parole basically."

So, the Avenging Women were acting as parole officers and trying to bring me back in front of the Joint Commission for not upholding my end of the deal by not working as a Coordinator for too long. I needed to go where they wouldn't think to. Where would the gods never think about going?

The Wastes.

"The gods would never go into the desert," I told Gavya.

Gavya stood up straight, pushing herself away from the walls of the building. "But the Wastes are so dangerous."

I shrugged. "And the Avenging Women and some pissed off gods are a walk in the park?"

Gavya started pacing. "But you have nothing. No food or water. You need those, apparently. And you have no way to stop somewhere and gather supplies."

"Yup," I said, more casually than I was actually feeling, "that is a problem. But that would be a problem anywhere I go. I really only have two options, the way I see it."

Gavya looked at me. Her eyes seemed concerned and almost slightly terrified, but willing to follow my lead. Inside, I was screaming at myself that I was crazy and really seriously going to end up dead, or worse. But she was looking at me, and I let my crazy mouth keep talking while my rational brain just shook its head.

"I have two options," I repeated, "I can stay here and let the Avenging Women take me." I looked at Gavya for a second and realized it wasn't just me anymore. "Well, now, take us. You removed books from the Annex. Pretty sure they can arrest you for that." Gavya blanched and nodded. "Or we can get outta Dodge. Wherever we go, we will not have any supplies either of us might need. It is going to be hard and probably will suck. But if we go far enough, fast enough, we may just buy ourselves enough time to make use of the books we stole and see if there is a way to put human me and spirit me back together again."

"And if we fix Humpty Dumpty," Gavya said slowly, while gesturing at me, "maybe a renewed spirit, body and soul of the strongest Heka user ever could force the gods to admit what they did. Maybe you could even get them to admit to why they did it and why they were scared of you in the first place."

"Is it worth the risk of fleeing to the most dangerous place in Taikarlu?" I asked Gavya.

She nodded. "The Wastes are not exactly part of Taikarlu, so to speak, but yes. It's worth the risk."

"You know Taikarlu better than I do." I told her. "Gavya, lead the way." As I talked, I could feel the heaviness of my limbs getting stronger. The Avenging Women were getting closer again. "And let's run, m'kay?" I said the last part so causally, Gavya missed the panic I felt until I grabbed her arm, pushed her in front of me and yelled, "For the love of all the gods, I said run!"

Gavya stumbled slightly at first, but then caught on to my alarm. She took off like a shot, running between buildings, down side streets, and crossing roads. As we ran, the feeling of the paralyzing power of the Avenging Women started to slacken. But then, we turned a corner between a pastry shop and a row of townhomes. The feeling of concrete muscles slammed back into me, and I grabbed the back of Gavya's top, yelling out, "Nope! Not this way." I just barely caught sight of the white flowing hair of an Avenging Woman as Gavya and I turned around and sprinted to run the other way.

The Avenging Women seemed to be everywhere. I don't know if there had always been this many of them, wandering the streets of Taikarlu and I just had never noticed before, or if they were all just out looking for me, but it started to make me panic. Several more times, Gavya would turn down a street, and I would know there was an Avenging Woman that way. Whenever I began to feel them closing in again, I would yell that to Gavya and we would immediately turn around and back-track until the feeling lessened again. Then, Gavya would turn somewhere else to cut through a different courtyard, or go in the front door of one building and out the back again, then cross some road and cut through a park. My internal Taikarlu-GPS got messed up from so many detours that I lost track of where I was. But Gavya seemed ever sure that she knew exactly where she was going.

In time, we left the warmth of the perpetual summer. The Central Hub Business District faded away and soon we were running through streets lined with daffodils and tulips, a light misty rain falling on us. The feeling of the Avenging Women slacked off significantly here, but Gavya and I knew we still weren't safe. Old Town was mostly populated by the gods and we couldn't be sure which ones were calling out the warrant on me. At any moment, we could turn a corner and run smack into whoever had set the Women on me in the first place. Then, all it would take is for them to whistle up a Tim and the Avenging Women would know exactly where we were. And that was assuming that the tracker in the Ward, if there was one, wasn't already telling them.

By the time we reached the middle of River Run, my lungs felt like they were on fire. The cool, crisp air helped some, but I needed to stop. I sped up slightly and pulled on the fabric of Gavya's saree. She stopped and turned to me.

"What is it?" she asked, barely even panting.

"Stop," I wheezed. "I need to stop." I bent over and put my hands on my knees, trying to catch my breath. I waved an arm up and down my body. "Mostly human, remember?"

"Oh," was all Gavya said. "Well, River Run has the most restaurants of anywhere in Taikarlu. Maybe we can take a few minutes to grab some food and water for you."

While I panted and wiped sweat from my brow, Gavya looked around. She spotted a food truck across the street from us, and pointed. "There. What should I get?"

I was pulling the collar of my shirt off my chest, using it to fan myself. Air movement helped me cool off. Apparently, all the paper of the scrolls I had shoved in my shirt acted like insulation, holding my body heat close to me. I thought for a second, then answered her.

"Water, a lot of water, or anything wet to drink if they don't have water. And food. Not anything that can spoil, but like bags of chips, or trail mix or something."

Gavya sprinted across the street, while I sat on the pavement watching her. I had never been to River Run before and it was actually quite pretty. The trees had leaves in a million vibrant shades of red, gold and purple. The grass was brilliant green underneath piles of leaves that somehow, even though they had all turned brown, still seemed to shimmer. Beyond the food truck, I could see the river. The water bubbled down its path, seeming to both laze along and gurgle quickly at the same time. It was crystal clear, blue and white, and the thin shore line was perfectly white, soft sand. Further down the river, there were stone bridges crossing its path. The whole scene looked like the perfect place to bring a picnic and a good book and just relax.

But Gavya and I did not have time to enjoy it for long. The muscles in my legs began to tense. Either I ran too fast without stretching first or the Avenging Women were catching up. I called out to Gavya and she came trotting back to me.

"We need to go." I told her.

"Wait," she countered, "I convinced the man at the food truck to let me borrow his back pack. Give me the books from your shirt." I took all the scrolls shoved in my clothing out and handed them over. Gavya hurriedly pushed them all into a large pocket of the backpack and zipped it shut. Then she began to open another pocket, showing me its contents. "Is what I got ok?"

The cramping in my legs was getting worse and spreading to my arms. It wasn't just shin splints causing my pain. I put out a hand to stop her questions. "No time, they're coming."

Gavya reached into the pocket she had been opening, pulled out a bottle of water, then zipped it closed again, slinging the bag on her back. "Later, then." She shoved the water at me. "But for now, this. Drink."

I took the water, opened it, and gulped it down. Drinking it made me feel better.

"Ready now?" Gavya asked. I nodded and she took off. I followed, wishing I could really stop, but knowing I couldn't. I don't like running and I had done a lot of it already.

River Run did not gently turn into the Hills, but did so all at once. The gentle rolling meadows suddenly became hills that were hard to climb. The uneven ground was all at once slick and treacherous. My sneakers did not help with traction on the snow and ice that just suddenly coated everything. And worst of all, it was cold! My skin began to tingle and my teeth chatter. I was shivering and it is hard to shiver and run at the same time. Especially when you have been running for so long that you have been sweating. Sweat and cold are not a fun combo. Once again, I reached out and grabbed Gavya's saree.

She turned back and looked at me, shock on her face. "Oh Bella!" she cried, "Oh, darling, you are freezing." Gavya began to unwrap her saree.

"What are you doing?" I asked her through chattering teeth.

Gavya tsked at me. "I am not somewhat human. The cold won't bother me." She continued unwrapping the layers of her saree. "It might not be quite decent, but never mind. I will be fine in my choli and petticoat. Here." Gavya walked over to me and started draping the loose fabric around me like a blanket. She rubbed my arms. "Better?"

Actually, I was better. A lot better, in fact. The fabric that had seemed so light and flowy on Gavya felt like a warm fleece blanket around me. I nodded, and slowly my teeth stopped clacking so hard. "Ready to go again?" Gavya eyed me like a mother hen would one of her chicks.

I shifted the saree/blanket so I could hold it around myself easier while moving. "Ready," I replied. When Gavya twisted her mouth and looked at me through the side of her eyes, as if she didn't quite believe me, I stood up straighter. "Really, not even shivering now, promise."

Gavya began running again, but changed her pace. Instead of moving at top speed, Gavya went slower. Fast enough to move quickly out of the Hills, but slow enough I wouldn't excessively sweat and get chilled again.

As quickly as River Run changed to the Hills, the Hills became the Wastes. Roads and sidewalks just dissolved into nothing. Homes and buildings were just gone. Where there had been plants and trees and flowers, now there was vast emptiness. A sea of rough, gritty sand and a constant wind, just strong enough to tug at clothing and pull whisps of hair from their ponytails. And it was hot. Not the perfect warmth of the Business District but a heat that made the skin feel too tight.

I was sweating under the saree/blanket again, and this time it was a sticky sweat that did nothing to cool me. Gavya stopped running. She had to. There was no running in this loose, drifting sand. The Wastes reminded me of documentaries I had seen of the Sahara Desert. I pulled off the saree/blanket and gave it back to Gavya with my thanks for keeping me warm.

Gavya set down the backpack and took a moment to rearrange her saree back over her undergarments. I looked past her and saw that the nothingness went on past the horizon.

"How far should we go?" I asked her.

"How hungry are you right now?" Gavya asked back.

Confused, I asked Gavya what one had to do with the other.

"Well," she replied, "my suggestion is to go until we can't see the Hills anymore or until you can't wait to eat anymore, whichever comes first."

That was a plan that made sense, and I told her so. "Right now, I am more thirsty than hungry I think, but I need to ration whatever water you happened to get. So, I think, for now, let's just go until I say stop? Unless, you may eventually need a break?"

Gavya waved me off. "Not human," she said flippantly. "You set the pace and now I will follow you." She outstretched an arm, gesturing for me to lead the way. I picked a direction directly opposite the way back into the Hills and set off, and Gavya followed.

Walking through the desert Wastes was not easy, especially after having spent hours running through every other part of the city of Taikarlu. I was hot, sweaty and felt all-around gross, but I forced myself to keep going. Every time I looked back, the Hills got smaller and smaller in the distance. Keeping the Hills in back of me was the only way I kept us walking in the same direction. The sun in the Wastes was the same as in Taikarlu, always at the zenith, bright and relentless.

By the time the Hills were just a speck on the horizon, I could not go any further. My mouth was dry and my tongue felt thick. My skin was hot and I could feel it blistering and starting to peel. I signaled to Gavya that it was time to call it quits. Every muscle in my legs was protesting.

"Finally," Gavya sighed and unceremoniously plopped down in the sand.

"I thought you didn't get tired," I teased.

Gavya looked at me and rolled her eyes. "Tired? No. Bored? Yes. I am a book person who loves reading about interesting places, getting lost in them in my mind. All I have seen for hours was sand, sand, and, wait for it, more sand!"

I chuckled at her. Most of the time, it was annoying to have everyone around you have no real needs while you did. But Gavya's lack of basic emotions in a hard situation, like being bored instead of hungry, made for comical relief. Speaking of hungry, my stomach decided to make its protestations of abuse clear as I sat down next to Gavya.

Gavya slung the backpack onto the ground in front of her and pulled a wad of texts from it. She shoved the bag at me. "Eat, drink, while I sort out this mess we made. My poor, pretty papers, what have we done to you?"

I took the bag and opened the large pocket that didn't contain the books and scrolls. Inside, I found bags of plain potato chips (ugh), beef jerky (double ugh), trail mix and water. All the chocolates in the trail mix had melted into a gooey mess, coating all the other nuts and dried fruit in its soup (triple ugh). If I had to eat, which I did, I figured it was best to get the grossest things eaten first so that when I was more tired and less happy about my conditions, I would at least have more preferable food. Messy chocolate coated trail mix it was. I counted out the bottles of water. There were six of them. I figured I should be safe drinking half a bottle every time we thought I needed water. I have no idea how I came up with the number, since we had no clue how long we had to be in the Wastes or what else could possibly happen while we were here. But it was a form of rationing, so I went with it.

While I ate and rested, Gavya shuffled the scrolls and books around, looking first at one then at another. From time to time, she would grumble or mutter under her breath. Sometimes, I could catch what she was saying. Most of it was along the lines of "Eww, sweat stains" or "So wrinkled, why did I shove this in my waistband?" Other times, there were exclamations that made me think she was on to some idea or another of how to get us out of this predicament. Those were usually followed up with grunts of frustration, indicating that the line of thought she had been following hit a dead end.

Finally, I finished off the gross trail mix and almost half a bottle of water. I walked a couple of paces away from Gavya, dug a hole in the sand, and took care of some other basic human necessities. There was literally nothing but flat desert for miles, so privacy was definitely in short supply. Embarrassed or not, I had to do what I had to do. Thankfully, Gavya was too engrossed with the books to even notice.

With that finished, I returned to Gavya and used the remaining bit of my ration of water to rinse my hands and scrub my face. I had no soap, so it was just the illusion of cleaning, but something is better than nothing.

Once my hands were dry, which only took seconds in the Wastes' heat, I sat next to Gavya and pulled over a scroll she had recently abandoned. "What do we got?"

"Nothing." She huffed, slapping down the book she had been reading. "A great, big, fat nothing."

I looked at her and saw exasperation. Gavya was now as stuck in this problem as I was. If we couldn't figure out how to put my halves back together before the gods or the Avenging Women found us, I would not be the only one going before the Joint Commission for crimes. Gavya had stolen from the Annex. She had abandoned her duties without leave or replacement, leaving the Annex unguarded. She had allowed an unregistered user in the restricted section, and worst of all, she was aiding and abetting a known wanted person. No matter what the gods tried to say my crimes were, hers were enough that, if found guilty, she could get put in the Taikarlu prison for a long, long time. And I knew from experience, that was a very unpleasant place to be.

"Start simple." I tried to soothe her. "What is our first priority?"

Gavya sighed and closed her eyes. "I guess it would be to put you back together. If we do that, then we can prove that the gods did not honor the agreement first, and any actions you, and by extension I, took were in self-defense."

I thought on that for a moment. To put myself back together, according to the little bit I had read, I needed to find my body in the human world while it was sleeping. But the Ward prevented my spirit from going to the human world. To top that off, I had no idea where my body was, how old it was, and in what state it was in. For all I knew, my physical body could be eighty years old, in a hospital, dying.

"I think." I said slowly. "I think our first goal is to find out where my body is and what's going on with it. We can't figure out anything else with reconnecting my two parts until we know that."

Gavya cocked her head to the side, considering this. "You told me you heard your old teachers once when you passed out, right?"

I nodded. "Yeah, from what my teacher was saying, my body was probably unconscious too."

"So," Gavya said slowly, a small sly smile forming on her face, "the best way for you to connect with your body is probably when you are unconscious."

I considered this. "As far as we can tell, with the Ward in place, it may be the only way my spirit and my body can at least come close." I paused and ran it all through my mind again. "Yeah, being unconscious, not asleep but actually unconscious, is our best lead so far for reconnecting the body and spirit."

Gavya laughed, low in her throat, and shook her head. "Sorry, Bella."

Confused, I asked what Gavya was sorry for.

Gavya again just shook her head. "Just know I'm sorry for this. Really, really sorry, Bella."

I started to think that whatever Gavya was saying she was sorry for, she couldn't have actually felt too bad about because she continued to have a mischievous grin. But before I could complete that thought, a sharp pain formed in my temple and spots floated in my eyes. Between the constant pain in my Warded arm, the exhaustion from running for my life, the rationing of water and food, and Gavya's help, I went down like a rock. My last thought before the world went black was that Gavya enjoyed punching me a little too much.

Anna Part One

"Stand back guys." Mrs. Campbell said. The boys laughed again and started to pull out their phones. "If y'all even think about recording her, you will be suspended, I guarantee it." Mrs. Campbell's warning made them stop pulling out their cellphones but didn't stop their laughter. "Anna?" Anna felt a hand touch her shoulder, shaking it gently. "Anna, can you hear me, sweetie?"

Anna groaned as she came back to consciousness. It had happened again, and this time in school, during class. Anna took stock of her body. She had fallen when she passed out, she could tell, but the only parts of her that hurt were her left hip and wrist. They didn't hurt too bad. Carefully, she flexed both and gauged their injury level. No super sharp pains, no stiffness, probably just bruised. One more mental check of her body and Anna was relieved that, at least this time, she hadn't wet herself. It's bad enough to collapse in the middle of class, in front of everyone. It would have been worse if she had peed herself too.

Finally, Anna opened her eyes, much to Mrs. Campbell's relief. "I'm okay." Anna told her teacher as she started to sit up. Mrs. Campbell reached out a hand and helped Anna stand, guiding her to the nearest desk. Mrs. Campbell shooed the kid sitting at that desk out of the chair so she could have Anna sit in there.

"I'm going to call the office and have someone come get you, ok?" Mrs. Campbell said once Anna was settled. "They will call your mom for you."

Anna groaned again. "No, please, Mrs. Campbell, I'm fine." She pleaded. "Don't call my mom."

Mrs. Campbell had been walking towards the phone on the wall by her desk. She turned back to Anna, her eyes full of sympathy. "I'm sorry, honey, I have to. Your mom made a medical 504 plan with the school. It's a legally binding contract of what we have to do if you have any medical issues while here at school. The 504 says if you pass out, we have to call Mom. I have no choice, sweetie." The teacher continued to the phone, and called the office.

Anna knew from past experience that she had about ten minutes before someone from the office, probably the school secretary Mr. Arnold, would come down and get her, saying her mom would be there soon to pick her up. Then Mom would take her home, fret and worry over her, calling the doctors, and making her rest even though Anna always felt fine after she passed out.

Anna packed up her belongings while Mrs. Campbell got the class settled back down. Right as Mrs. Campbell started talking about Shakespeare's Sonnet eighteen again, Mr. Arnold poked his head through the classroom door, pointed at Anna, and signaled for her to come. Anna grabbed her stuff and tried to exit the class without causing more disruptions. She failed, of course, tripping over the trashcan on her way out, making it clatter and bang around before finally spilling all its contents at Mrs. Campbell's feet.

Red with embarrassment, again, Anna tried to shift her book bag and bent down to pick up the trashcan and put the trash back into it, but ended up just making her book bag slide up her back and knock into her head. The other kids in the class, who had just stopped laughing at Anna for passing out, started up again. There was no way the teacher would calm them down this time. Mrs. Campbell gave Anna a pitiful look before waving her off. "Just go, sweetie. I'll get that. Hope you feel better."

Anna sighed and walked away from her mess. What is wrong with me lately, she thought as she followed Mr. Arnold to the office. I've never been exactly graceful, but dang, I can't do anything anymore without being just plain awkward.

Anna tried not to think about how upside-down everything in her life had become as she walked to the office. Once she entered through the big glass doors in the center of her high school that led to the secretaries', principal's and guidance counselors' offices, she knew what she would find.

Right on cue, there she was, Anna's mother, yet again arguing with the principal that maybe Anna should be changed to a home-bound student. Home-bound meant you were too sick to attend regular school with everyone else and that teachers would come to your home several times a week to give you mini-class lessons for each class you were enrolled in and then leave you work to do over the next several days when you felt well enough. Everyone had told Mom that Anna didn't need that, everyone. The doctors, the guidance counselors, the principal, even Anna herself, but Mom wouldn't listen. Anna's mom was a lawyer and wasn't used to losing arguments.

There are those words again, Anna thought, "used to." Everything in my life is now broken up into used to and now what is. Anna let her mind dive deep into remembering everything while her mom finished arguing with, and losing to, the principal.

Anna's life used to be weird, but a good weird. Her mom, Julia McIntosh, had been a pre-law major in her bachelor's degree when she met Anna's father, Nick Cain. The two had been friends as Julia finished law school and Nick worked as some sort of prosecuting attorney. They were both only children who had lost their parents and had bonded closely. Once Julia had secured a job at a prestigious human rights law firm, they had agreed they both wanted to have a child but not the romantic relationship that went along with it. So, they made a pact to do it together, drew up legal documents assigning rights and responsibilities, and went to a clinic to have invitro fertilization. AnnaBella Cain was that child, and she used to love her life. Her parents were friends, always platonic and completely cordial with each other when she was growing up, but were great parents, sharing the joys and responsibilities of raising Anna.

Julia and Nick had always put AnnaBella first. The only place they never could agree was on her name. Julia wanted to name her Anna and Nick wanted to name her Bella. To compromise, they smushed the names together and each nicknamed their daughter what they preferred. But Anna had not been called Bella by anyone in months now.

Everything used to be great. Julia used to be this high-powered lawyer jet setting around the world in spike high heels and power suits, defending those who couldn't defend themselves. She had always seemed to Anna to be in control and in charge. Tall, slender, with long reddish-brown hair and beautiful skin, smart and dedicated, Julia used to be the epitome of classy, but was always also down-to-earth with a sensible car and a hundred-year-old Craftsman home.

Nick used to be the complete opposite. Tall and, Anna assumed, gorgeous, Nick looked like a Mediterranean model with his muscular build, olive skin and hint of an accent. He used to be the complete opposite of Julia, dressing very casually, jeans and t-shirts but driving fast, expensive cars and living in a fashionable penthouse condo decorated like a magazine, with modernistic furniture and art everywhere.

Anna used to split her time between them, easily moving from one lifestyle to the other, loving her time equally with both. But her father used to be her favorite person in the whole world and Anna used to be excited for her senior year of high school because she was going to spend half her school day working with him at his job and earning class credit, and a paycheck, for it.

Now, nothing was what it used to be. Now, Anna's father was dead and her mother was a wreck. And Anna? Now, no one knew what was wrong with Anna. It happened the first day of summer vacation. Anna's father had picked her up from the last day of school, and took her to say goodbye to her mother, who would be spending the entire summer traveling the world for her job. Anna was supposed to spend the summer interning with her father in preparation for her upcoming co-op position. According to what she was told later, Anna and her father left her mother's house and headed into the city for dinner.

But before they could get to the restaurant, their car was t-boned by a drunk driver. Anna was thrown from the car, her seatbelt malfunctioning at that crucial moment. From what her mother said, this malfunction actually saved Anna's life because after she was ejected, the car caught fire somehow and her father died in the flaming wreckage.

Anna had to be told everything that happened because she had no memory of anything after meeting her dad outside of the school that day. Apparently, she had spent the rest of June, July and August in a coma no one could explain. She had injuries, of course. There was some bruising here and there, a little road rash, and some broken ribs, but all in all the doctors had counted her extremely lucky. That is, until they couldn't wake her up for almost three months.

The doctors had run test after test. Anna had brain activity, a lot of it actually. There was no swelling or bleeding, or anything else the doctors could point to as the cause of the coma. But Anna just wouldn't wake up.

Julia had spent almost every moment of those three months at her daughter's bedside. The only times she left was when she was taking care of Nick's final affairs, dealing with the insurance, his funeral and selling his condo. Julia had all of Nick's artwork and possessions put into storage so that if Anna... no, not if, when... when Anna woke up, she could choose what of her father's she wanted to keep and the rest could be sold and the money put into a trust that would keep Anna financially comfortable for the rest of her life.

Of course, Anna did wake up. The doctors declared her healthy rather quickly and sent her home. They had no choice. All of their tests said that Anna could not have just been in a coma for three months, but must be a healthy, active teenager. In fact, if someone read the tests reports without knowing Anna's circumstances, they would have thought that she had spent the summer training to do a marathon rather than lying unconscious in a hospital bed. The doctors could not make heads or tails of it, so they just sent her home and wished her the best.

That's when the seizures started, and the arm pain. Anna's neurologist called her passing-out episodes seizures but, in reality, had to admit she had no idea why Anna was passing out. Again, the tests were baffling. EEGs, MRIs, the works, Anna had had it all. And still they had no answers.

The same was true for her arm. After coming home from the hospital, Anna began to get sharp, radiating pain in her right arm. There had never been any injury to her right side from the car accident. After running every test they could think of and, again, coming up empty-handed, the neurologist declared that the arm pain must be associated with the seizures she guessed were Anna's problem. Except the arm pain and the passing out did not always happen at the same time. Since the doctors couldn't figure anything out at all, they just ignored that and kept giving her treatments for seizures. Treatments that didn't work.

Julia used to be put together and classy, but now, with a daughter who almost died and had medical issues no one could figure out, Julia was a wreck. She still wore the in-charge clothes, but they no longer looked as badass on her. Her beautiful hair that used to be always on point, styled professionally, was now usually slung in messy ponytail. She used to jet-set around the world, and now the only time Julia rushed anywhere, it was usually to a doctor or emergency room with Anna in tow.

Anna stood at the side of her mother, listening as she and the principal rehashed the same arguments they had been having for months. Eventually, Mom gave up and turned to Anna.

"Anna, baby, c'mon. Let's get you home so you can rest," Julia took Anna's bags from her.

Anna tried to reason with her. "Mom, I'm fine. I don't need to go home and rest. I feel…" But Mom was already walking away with Anna's bookbag on one arm, while she dug through her purse to find her car keys. Sighing at not being listened to again, Anna just followed. The principal may be able to win against her mother's courtroom tactics, but Anna felt like she never could.

So, off she went. Back home to miss more classes while she laid in bed and her mother brought her tea and toast, insisting Anna sleep when she had no desire to. Anna pulled out her cellphone and texted Ben.

Ben was Anna's friend, her only friend this year. Last year, Anna had been okay with only having one friend, Lila. Anna had never been popular, and most people in her school had excluded her for not being into all the fashion and sports and groupie type stuff they all thought was so cool. Lila and Anna had agreed long ago that most of the preppy, cheerleader stuff was crap, and had become best friends easily. But Lila had graduated and was off in Scotland having wonderful adventures at college. When Anna had finally started school this year, two weeks late, she was ostracized even further. No one wanted to be friends with the weird kid who would just suddenly drop on the floor for no reason. No one had wanted to be friends with the kid whose dad died in a fiery wreck they just barely escaped and whose mom had become overbearingly protective.

No one but Ben, at least. Ben and his grandfather had been living in the northeastern part of the U. S. with his parents until they died in a car accident last summer. Now, he and his grandfather lived here in the Midwest with his sister and brother-in-law. Ben had also been in the accident that killed his parents, apparently, and it had left burns that looked like splashes on him. Ben shied away anytime anyone asked him about the accident, and Anna just let it be. She could understand not wanting to talk about the horrible car accident that changed your whole life. It was like the two of them had come to a mutual agreement without ever really even needing to say it out loud. If Ben didn't want to talk about what happened, she wouldn't make him, and in return, he wouldn't ask her about her dad.

Ben had missed the first few weeks of school, just like Anna, because of the move and because of his injuries. They found each other when they both started as new in classes that everyone else was already comfortable in. They bonded over having to play catch up and teachers who didn't understand how hard it was to try to learn class material in a few days, material everyone else had been able to take weeks to learn, while still trying to keep up with the new stuff along with everyone else. Ben and Anna had laughed over their shared state of being perpetually one step behind.

Now, Ben and Anna had formed basically a support group for each other. The weird freaks who had weird medical stuff and were always missing school for doctor's appointments and whatnot. They ate lunch together, walked to classes together and basically hung out whenever they were in the school building. A bully might take on Anna alone, or even maybe Ben alone. But together? Ben's 6'5" muscular frame and Anna's lawyer parent-inspired mouth were too much for a bully to take on all at once. Whenever Ben missed school, Anna would go to his classes and collect his missed work for him, and Ben would do the same for her. They would get that work to the other one so that it could be turned in on time, and neither of them would fail as badly.

Thus, when Mom made her go home for rest she didn't need, Anna texted Ben to collect the rest of her assignments for the day. He used to offer to bring the assignments to Anna's house immediately after school, but they both soon learned that would be pointless. Mom would just keep the work downstairs and insist Anna should rest and worry about school later. Instead, Ben would meet Anna at his locker the next day and give her the assignments, usually giving her the answers for the work in classes they shared as well. Technically, it was cheating, but the two didn't care. School was not designed for the chronically ill and they both were just trying to survive it the best they could.

Anna waited until they got home to try to debate with her mother about making her rest. As soon as they got into the house, Mom started in. "Anna, now, go up to your room, get some comfy pj's on and I will be up soon with something to eat."

"Moommm." Anna whined. "Can't I just lie on the couch and watch TV? I feel fine, really."

Julia turned from setting her and Anna's bags down on the kitchen counter, and looked at her daughter. Her face was a cross between frustration and concerned sympathy. "Anna, baby, the doctor says you should rest after a seizure, not play on your phone and watch TV. Go upstairs." Mom held out one hand and Anna, knowing what her mother wanted, handed her cellphone over.

But that didn't stop her from continuing to grumble. "You know, it's November. In four months, I'll be eighteen and you won't be able to tell me what to do anymore. Why don't you ever listen to me?"

"Anna!" Mom cried out, losing all of the concerned sympathy.

"I am only trying to help you, to get you better! You think I like being like this? I wish I could let you just run free and do everything a normal teen does. But you are not a normal teen anymore. Don't you know that?"

Anna turned away from her mother to do as she said, but still muttered under her breath. "I know I'm not normal. How could I not? You remind me every day." Still muttering to herself about how unfair it all was, Anna went up to her room and pretended to rest.

Anna must have actually napped because she woke up to her room dark even though the curtains were open. She didn't remember falling asleep, but she did remember dreaming. In her dreams, a beautiful woman in a saree was reading books to her and calling her Bella. Anna and the woman seemed to be arguing about whether Anna had a body, Anna insisted she did while the other woman insisted she didn't.

Anna's right arm was hurting. A lot, and Anna didn't feel very good. Her mouth felt dry, her tongue thick. She tried to call out for her mom but Anna's throat felt too scratchy to yell. Since Mom had taken her phone, all she could do was go downstairs to get her.

Anna got out of bed and stood up. Immediately, she felt dizzy and hot. The world closed in around her, black spot floating in front of her eyes. Anna tried to step forward, but it felt like her foot went straight through the floor and she fell.

"So, in further research on dehydration, apparently an over-consumption of caffeine can speed up the process, so I thought I would come check on…
Woah, you don't look good."
"Yeah, thanks for that," I tried to say, but apparently my tongue was not cooperating.
Gavya knelt down and put her hand on my forehead. It felt very cooling. She tsked, and said "Your skin is very dry and your head is warm. Do you have a

headache, feel bad in any way?"
I nodded yes, since my mouth didn't
work.
Gavya rocked back on her heels,
thinking, "Huh. You must actually be
getting dehydrated. That means water
would be a need for you. But how?"
She sat there, staring into space, still
thinking to herself.
I poked her, and she looked at me
again. "Oh crap!" she exclaimed,
"Yeah, water. I'll get you water."

Anna heard footsteps pounding up the stairs as she tried to pick herself up off the floor. Mom came bursting into Anna's room. "I heard a thump, Anna. Are you ok?" Mom noticed her on the floor and gasped. "Oh, sweetie, not again. Twice in one day?" Mom reached down and helped Anna back into bed.

Anna, gestured to her mother to hand her the tea that was sitting on her nightstand. Once she drank some, Anna's mouth stopped feeling quite so parched. "Thanks," she said roughly, "and no, Mom, not twice in one day. This was…different." Anna could not find the words to explain what had happened. Her brain felt foggy and she had a headache developing behind her eyes.

Mom rubbed Anna's forehead, pushing her hair out of her eyes, but then stopped. "Oh, Anna, you're burning up. And your skin feels so dry." It worried Anna that her mother described the way she felt the same way that the woman in her vision had described it. But with her brain playing keep-away with her thoughts, Anna could not find the right words to tell her mom.

Before Anna could make a coherent thought to explain to her mother the weirdness of what had occurred, Mom was on the phone with the doctor's office, listing every symptom and demanding they see Anna right away because "whatever is wrong with her is obviously getting worse."

Mom had the phone on speaker, so Anna could hear the nurse

on the other end of the line asking her mother how high Anna's fever was and all the normal questions they would ask a parent of a sick kid. The nurse was patiently explaining to the increasingly panicked Mom that even kids with seizure disorders and brain injuries can get normal illnesses like the cold and that there was no reason to suspect that wasn't what Anna had.

Anna reached out to her mother, who was pacing the bedroom while talking on the phone, and grabbed her shirtsleeve as she paced by. "Mom," Anna began, "calm down. I'm fine, I swear. I just feel a little dehydrated. Maybe I just didn't drink enough water today or something."

Mom finally turned to look at her daughter, mid-berating of a nurse for not taking this seriously enough. Anna continued, "Look, Mom," Anna took a large swig of the now cold tea, "better. I feel loads better. Just dehydrated."

The disembodied voice of the nurse came from the phone. "Dehydration can happen pretty easily, and would cause all those symptoms you described. Something to drink and some food would go a long way to fixing the issue. Call back if her fever goes over 102 or if the symptoms don't resolve in twelve hours." Then the nurse escaped by hanging up on Mom.

Anna could not escape as easily as the nurse, though, and had to continue convincing her mother that she really, really was okay, just thirsty. Dubious, Mom went to the kitchen and grabbed Anna a sports drink and some soup. Bringing it back up, Mom watched as Anna finished both. Then she checked her forehead, noting Anna had cooled down a bit.

"Can you admit maybe you went just a teeny, tiny bit overboard, Mom?" Anna asked once Mom seemed satisfied Anna was on the mend.

Her mother started to look cross again, "Anna, you don't understand. You been so sick..."

"Not sick, Mom." Anna said forcefully. "I have not been sick. I was in a car accident. I got hurt and somethings don't seem to be working right for me anymore. But that's not sick, Mom."

Mom rolled her eyes and huffed. "Fine, not sick. Weak..."

"Mmmm, nope." Anna interrupted her mother, finally feeling like she might win at least an inch from her. "All the tests said I am not weak. Even when I woke up from the coma, the doctors said my muscles weren't as atrophied as they expected them to be. So, not weak either, Mom."

"So, what have you been, Anna?" Mom gritted her teeth. "What? What were you that kept me out of work for almost four months? What are you that has me being called by your school at least twice a week to come get you? What would you call it, then?"

Anna opened her mouth to give a biting retort, but then stopped herself. Her mother was looking at her, listening to her for the first time since June. Now was not the time to get into a pissing contest with her. But it was the time to maybe make Mom realized how overboard she had gone with trying to care for and protect Anna.

"Mom," Anna started again, slowly this time. "I absolutely love you and know you love me. I cannot imagine how scary all of this has been for you. Watching your kid in a hospital for months, not knowing what was wrong, sucked way more than I could imagine, I know. But now, now I am not sick, I am not weak, I am weird. And you keep treating me like I will break any minute."

Anna took a deep breath, trying to stay calm and speak rationally. "But I won't. The stuff that is happening, the passing out, my arm, it's just weird. The doctors can't find anything dangerous or life threatening. Hell, they can't find anything at all. So, maybe, Mom, just a little bit... back off? I am almost an adult. Let me decide if there is something wrong, and how wrong that something is? Let me say what I can handle and what I can't? It's my body and only I know how I feel."

"Weird," Mom muttered, looking down at the bed. She sat down on the corner of the mattress and started picking at the comforter. "Weird." Mom said the word a little louder, as if testing how it felt in her mouth. "That's how you would describe all of this? Weird? Just weird?"

"Yeah." Anna tried to make her voice as soothing as possible. Mom was used to being in charge of everything, all the time, as a lawyer. When the accident happened, Julia had just transferred that in-charge attitude to Anna's care. Anna knew it was a big step just for Mom to acknowledge that Anna would have a different idea about it all, and to accept that.

Mom sighed, long and loud. "Weird." She muttered again, shaking her head. She sighed one more time. "Ok, I can try to back off. Let you decide if you need to come home when things happen at school rather than just insist on it. Ask you how you feel instead of just assuming, I guess."

"Thank you." Anna replied as Mom headed out of the room, carrying away Anna's dirty dishes.

Mom stopped at the door and turned back. "But," Mom wagged her finger at Anna, "if you start getting worse, I will put my foot down, do you understand? No dumb or reckless choices, ok?"

Anna smiled. "Of course, Mom, I know you can't back off that much."

Mom stepped back into the room and gave Anna a hug with her free hand. "Oh, my baby, stop growing up. I thought," Mom sniffled, "I thought I would at least have your dad to lean on while you grew up and we had to start letting go and letting you live your own life. He would be so proud of you, you know that?"

Anna's eyes filled with tears as she shook her head. Mom never talked about Dad since the accident. "I miss him."

"Me too, baby." Mom's voice was heavy with tears she wasn't crying. "You just saw me and him as your mom and dad, but before you were born, he was my best friend. I miss my friend, like you miss your dad."

The two sat there, hugging each other and not speaking, for several minutes. Neither of them really cried, even though they both had wet eyes. They just sat there feeling their feelings for a bit. There really hadn't been time to talk about their grief with all of Anna's issues. Anna had missed her father's funeral and everything because of the coma. This was the first time the two really had acknowledged the loss that was mixed up in both of their reactions to Anna's health.

Finally, Mom stood back up, wiped her face, and headed to the door. "Get some rest, Anna." She started to say, but then paused remembering their agreement. "I mean, um, well, do you want to come downstairs, rest on the couch, and watch TV with me? If you feel up to it?"

Anna gave her mom a watery smile. "Sure, in a minute."

Anna Part Two

First thing the next morning, Anna went to her locker to retrieve her missing work from Ben. Ben was waiting there for her. It was easy to spot him in the crowds, his tall frame towering over all the other students. As she approached, Ben was leaning against the lockers. He was wearing his normal outfit of a tee-shirt over a long-sleeve turtleneck shirt and long athletic pants that covered all his burns. He finished off the look with a backpack slung off one shoulder, his right hand holding a blue folder out to her.

"Your work, ma'am." Ben said, smiling slightly.

Anna took the folder and started flipping through the pages inside. Some of them were worksheets with math problems and some were just lined paper with a hastily scribbled note, saying "read pages 185-216 in the text, be ready for a quiz on Friday." Anna noticed there was nothing from advanced biology, one of the classes Ben and Anna were actually in together. The advanced biology teacher, Ms. Eberrake, never let either of them off with easy work when they missed for medical stuff. Ben and Anna both swore she actually would have given them harder makeup work if she could have gotten away with it. Anna asked Ben why the work from that class was missing.

Ben pushed off the locker to stand straight up, holding one finger up in the air. "Ah, see, that's the fun part. Yesterday, in bio, we started the section on genetics. In Ms. Eberrake's infinite wisdom, she thought that the best way to teach us was to pair us up into groups of two and have us genetically design our own baby."

Anna's eyes grew wide. "What?"

Ben pulled a thick packet of papers out of his bag and handed them to Anna. "We have to use the rules of genetics, as contained in this packet, and our own looks, to make Punnett Squares of what a child with me as the father and you as the mother might look like. Everyone else did it in class yesterday. You and I will get to do it 'in our spare time' and turn it in Friday."

"Oh, for Pete's sake." Anna flipped through the packet. "This is stupid. When are we supposed to do this?"

Ben shrugged. "I guess our spare time would be after school. You could come over and we could do it at my house?" Ben said this almost jokingly, knowing Anna's mom would never go for it, but hoping they could do something the easy way for once.

Anna paused, thinking about what Mom would say to her going over to Ben's house after school. Last school year, Julia would have been ecstatic if Anna had said she was going over to a boy's house. Now, she wasn't so sure that Mom would react that way. Instead, Mom probably would worry about Anna 'overdoing it.'

But then Anna remembered the talk yesterday. Anna would just have to put her foot down and insist Mom trust that Anna would listen to her body. Anyway, it was just a homework assignment. It's not like Ben was inviting her over to climb Mt. Everest or practice running a marathon. She decided to call her mother at lunch and let her know she would be going to Ben's house after school to do the assignment. She wouldn't ask 'May I please" or 'Can I' but would just tell her mother, 'I am.' Or, she would try to, at least.

Anna spent the first half of the school day distracted by running a constant internal hype session in her mind, convincing herself that she could take charge in the conversation with Mom. By the time the lunch bell rang, she had gone over every possible conversation and argument she could think of in her head so many times, Anna was sure she had a logical counterpoint for any objections Mom might voice.

Feeling armed mentally, Anna went into the office and used the secretary's phone to call her mother at work. Her mother had forgotten to give Anna back her cell phone and, in her joy of Mom letting her watch TV instead of rest in her room, Anna forgot to ask for it. Because the caller ID on her work phone showed that it was the school calling, her mother must have assumed the call was about Anna having a medical issue again and answered before the phone finished the first ring.

"This is Julia, is Anna all right?" she said, impatiently.

"Mom, it's me," Anna replied, "you forgot to give me my cellphone back. Nothing's wrong but I need to go to Ben's house after school to work on a biology project. I will be home for dinner, ok?"

Anna drew a deep breath, waiting for the onslaught she was so sure was coming. All of her muscles were tensed as her body physically reacted to what she was sure would be a mental fight. She was so worked up she missed her mother's response entirely. It took her a full minute to realize her mother had spoken politely rather than yelled.

"Anna, you still there?" Mom asked. "Did you hear me?"

Feeling a little dazed, Anna asked her mom to repeat what she had said.

"I said have fun." Mom repeated.

Oh. That was not at all what Anna expected. In all her imagined scenarios, she had not once thought of what to do if her mom was as chill as she promised last night she would be. Anna stumbled over her words, thanking Mom and assured her that she would be home early. She got off the phone with her mother as quickly as possible, before Julia could change her mind.

Still dazed, Anna left the office and went to the lunchroom to let Ben know her mother had approved. Ben was just as disbelieving as Anna was. "She said have fun?" Ben asked repeatedly. "Just have fun? No long monologue about it? No why not at your house so she can watch you? Nothing?"

Anna shook her head at each of Ben's questions, repeating that Mom had just told her to "have fun." Ben finally believed Anna and just sat back, one French fry hanging out of his mouth like a toothpick, and said "Wow." Together, the two floated through the rest of their classes, excited that at least one of them had earned freedom from their families' medical captivity.

The two met at Ben's locker to walk to his house together at the end of the day. Ben finally asked Anna what she had done to get her mom to be so chill. Ben's sister, who was now his guardian, had never been as strict as Anna's mom, but she was still a lot more cautious of Ben's behaviors than either of them thought was necessary. Ben always gave his sister the benefit of the doubt, though. Between only being twenty-two herself, having parenting duties of a teenager and care of an elderly grandparent thrown at her unexpectedly at the same time as she lost both her parents, and having that teenager go from perfectly healthy to medically fragile in an instant was a lot to juggle at once, and Ben knew it. So, Ben thought, and Anna agreed that, if she messed up and was too overprotective sometimes, he had to cut her some slack.

Anna told Ben about her conversation with her mom the night before as they walked to his house. Ben's house was only a few blocks from the school, but the November chill made the walk seem longer. Ben grew unusually quiet when the pair turned the final corner down Borton Road towards his home.

Finally, Ben pointed to the driveway leading to a small, split-level house. "This is me." he stammered. Then he reached out his hand and grabbed Anna's elbow. "Wait." Ben rubbed his face, sighed and looked down, "I just... You know I live with my sister and her husband, right?" Anna nodded. "Well, my grandpa lives here too, and he can be... well... you know, very peculiar about some stuff. My sister and I, we love our heritage and culture and whatever. My brother-in-law is not Indigenous, but he has always respected our culture. Mom and Dad, they were big on teaching us everything, and my sister found a balance that respected our culture and her husband's. But Nummi can be a little set in the old ways, a little weird about it. It can be embarrassing sometimes." Ben looked at Anna with a slightly pleading face. "If he says something, don't think, I mean, don't make too much of it, ok?"

Anna smiled at Ben. "Family can be weird, don't worry about it. I'm sure your grandpa is fine."

Ben breathed a sigh of relief and let go of Anna's elbow. They walked into the house, and Ben called out. "Mari? I'm home." The front door of the house led to a set of stairs, half heading up and half heading down. They took the half heading up, and the stairs opened directly into the middle of the living room. To the right was another set of half stairs going up and a closed door. To the left was an arrangement of couches surrounding a television that was playing some cooking show on mute with the closed captioning on. Straight ahead was an open doorway, leading to the back of the house.

From somewhere in the back, Anna heard a light, musical voice call out, "Ben, yeah, how was your day?"

Ben walked to the closed door, which turned out to be a closet. He removed his warm outer gear and hung it up. He held out his hand, and Anna took off her coat for him to hang up too. While he did this, he responded to the voice. "Uh, good. Listen, my friend Anna is here. We need to work on a makeup assignment for class, ok?"

The voice came back. Anna realized it was coming from the open doorway. "Sounds good. Y'all want a snack or anything? I made banana bread." The voice seemed to be getting closer as it spoke until finally a very small, young woman came through the open door. She looked similar to Ben, except lithe and petite where he was bulky and tall. Anna realized this must be Ben's sister, Mari.

Mari reached over and hugged Ben, who had to almost fold in half to allow his sister to put her arms around his shoulders. He hugged her back, while she continued speaking. "Oh and say hello to Nummi." Mari jutted her chin toward the television, then when Ben rolled his eyes slightly, she playfully slapped his arm. "Tsk, be nice. Nummi loves you. He's crazy, but he loves you. And introduce your friend." At this, Mari looked at Anna and smiled. Anna smiled back shyly and gave a small wave.

Ben sighed again and walked over to the couches. Anna followed. There, Anna saw a very old version of Ben. The man had obviously at one time been strong and tall like Ben, but age had rounded his shoulders and softened his middle. Ben's hair was long, down his back to almost his waist, thick, and jet black and his eyes were a golden brown. The old man had long hair as well, past his shoulders, but what might have at one time been black was now gray and white, thin and wispy. His eyes were a muddier brown than Ben's but bore a piercing look that spoke to Anna of wisdom and remembrance.

Anna expected the man to show other signs of age when Ben began speaking to him. Slight confusion, or maybe a little hearing loss, a frailty in his voice even. But as Ben introduced Anna to his grandfather, she realized that the losses in his body in no way indicated a loss in his mind.

Ben's grandfather stood, somehow seeming to gather power back into himself as he did so and reached out his right hand to shake Anna's. His voice was quiet but strong as he said, smiling, "Hello, my dear. Call me Nummi. So nice to meet…" The old man's words trailed off and his smile faded as Anna took his offered hand. He looked down at their conjoined hands, then back up at Anna. His eyes took on a new light.

Nummi placed his left hand on top of both of their hands. "You have been ill, child, haven't you?"

Ben took a step back and interrupted. "Nummi, don't. Ugh, please don't be embarrassing."

Nummi ignored his grandson and continued looking at Anna, waiting. Anna answered him. "Well, yes. I was in a car accident in June, and…"

Ben interrupted again. "Anna, you don't have to tell him all that."

Nummi looked sharply at Ben. "Shh, grandson. Let her talk if she wants to." He turned to Anna again. "While not respectful about it, my grandson reminds me it may be impolite of me to ask. Please, only tell me if you wish."

Anna was startled and unsure, but one look into Nummi's eyes made her feel like telling him everything. She looked at Ben, who was becoming red in the face, and nervously shifting from one foot to another. "It's ok. I was in a car accident in June. My father died and I survived. But there have been a lot of things weird with me since."

Nummi lifted his left hand from Anna's and moved it to hover above her forehead. "May I?" he asked.

Anna nodded, not quite sure what he meant but somehow instinctively trusting him, and Nummi let his hand lower gently onto

Anna's head. His hand felt warm, warmer than she expected it to. Nummi closed his eyes and Anna heard a slight humming sound. She thought at first Nummi was the one humming, but then realized the sound was coming from inside her. Her body was humming, and she didn't even know why.

Nummi removed his left hand from Anna's head and let go of her hand with his right. The humming feeling inside of her stopped instantly. Nummi opened his eyes and stared directly into Anna's. "Your illness. It is not one doctors will ever solve. The doctors in hospitals, they don't know of this type of illness. It is not one they can fix with medicine or scans. I can help you." Nummi paused, glanced at Ben, and then back at Anna. "But I see from my grandson again that I forget that you do not know me or of our ways. I am making him ashamed. Forgive me." At this, Nummi sat back down on his couch and started watching the cooking show again.

Ben cleared his throat and stammered. "Let's go, um, let's go to the kitchen and grab a snack." He started walking away, looking at the floor and mumbling to himself.

Anna, bewildered and confused, instinctively followed him. Ben, with Anna behind him, walked through the open doorway that Mari had come out of. Mari must have disappeared to some other part of the house to give Ben and Anna privacy to work, because when Anna looked around the small but tidy kitchen and eat-in dining space, Mari was nowhere to be seen. There was warm banana bread, three loaves of it, sitting on the round, four-person table, and it smelled heavenly.

Ben sat down in one of the chairs and gestured for Anna to sit next to him. He explained as he sliced the banana bread. "Nummi has gotten into watching baking shows and Mari has picked up on it. Now, she is baking and cooking all sorts of things. I think she gets bored staying home with Nummi all day. She used to work, but she and Albert, that's my brother-in-law, worry about leaving Nummi home alone all day so she quit. Anyway, I'm sorry about Nummi. He can be a little…" Ben had said all this in a rush, not stopping to take a breath, while cutting and serving the banana bread. He pushed a slice in front of Anna and then bit into his own slice.

"Don't worry about it, Ben." she replied. "Honestly, I think it would be cool to talk to your grandpa. He probably has a lot of knowledge and stuff. You know, things most people don't think about nowadays. He seems kinda cool." Anna took a bite of the bread without thinking, and kept talking as she ate. "Hey, the doctors can't figure anything out, maybe he could oh my goodness, this is delicious." Anna interrupted herself and then just quit talking as she savored the bread that tasted as good as it smelled, better even.

Once she had finished her entire piece, she continued talking. "Anyway, like I was saying. One, your sister is an amazing cook. That was great. And two, don't worry about your grandpa. Should we just do the homework?"

Ben agreed and pulled the packet for biology out of his bookbag. The two then buckled down and worked on Punnett Squares for an hour. But Anna's mind kept floating back to what Nummi said. The doctors didn't know her illness. That much was true. Could Ben's grandfather know it, though? Could he maybe solve it?

Ben and Anna worked on their homework until Mari came into the kitchen to start prepping for dinner. Anna looked at the clock on the wall and realized it was after six. Mom would be pacing with worry.

Anna started gathering her things and shoving them in her bookbag. "I gotta get heading home. I promised Mom I wouldn't stay long."

Bed stood and stretched. "Oh man, I didn't even realize the time. Do you want me to get Albert to drive you home?"

Anna nodded. "Yeah, that'd be great. It's already getting dark."

Ben bounded off to find his brother-in-law. Anna, unsure what to do while she waited, noticed some family portraits on the wall between the living room and kitchen. She meandered slowly by the wall, looking at pictures of large groups of people, some of them so old they were black and white with yellowing edges hung next to ones that were newer and might have been Ben and Mari as children.

When she reached the door between the kitchen and the living room, Anna walked through it, finding even more family portraits. She was just circling the couch when her right arm started to hurt. Rubbing it, she willed the edges of her vision to stop going black.

"Now is not the time to pass out again," she whispered to

herself. "Please don't…"

"Sorry, Bella."
Confused, I asked what Gavya was sorry for.
Gavya again just shook her head, "Just know I'm sorry for this. Really, really sorry, Bella."
Pain bloomed in the middle of my cheek and I realized I was laying down in the sand. "What the hell did you do that for?"
Gavya laughed. "Well, it worked. You have been unconscious for a week in human time, Bella."
I sat up and started brushing sand from my hands and combing it out of my hair. "A week? No way. You just hit me, just now." Attempting to stand, I looked around for something to brace myself on, and saw a man. An old man with long white hair, tall but stooped from age. He was right there, his hand suddenly on my shoulder. But at the same time, he wasn't. I couldn't feel his hand and, somehow, I could almost see through him. The heat from the sand made him seem distorted, almost like a mirage.
"Who are you?" I asked.
"You shouldn't be here," he replied. "You belong with Anna. You need to come back to her."
I looked at the man, confused. "What? I am Anna. AnnaBella, that's my name. How could I not be with

myself?"
The man vanished as quickly as her
appeared. In the void where he had
been standing, I heard the words echo
again, "You shouldn't be here."

"Put a pillow under her head, I will call her mom." Anna heard Mari saying.

"Wait, no. Mari, I think she is ok. Anna?" Ben's voice was very close to Anna. She went through her mental checklist post-pass out. With nothing seeming out of place, besides being on the floor of Ben's living room, Anna opened her eyes.

Anna tried to speak, but her throat felt very dry. She coughed once to clear it and tried again. "Ben, I'm sorry. I must have overdone it."

As she looked up, Anna saw Ben sitting on the floor to her left and Nummi on her right. Nummi had his hand on her shoulder and his eyes were closed. He opened them quickly. Together, he and Ben helped Anna to sit up.

"Are you ok? Do you need some water?" Ben asked, seeming very concerned. Oh great, Anna thought, now Ben will treat me weird like everyone else does.

Anna struggled to sit upright further under her own power and curled her legs under herself. "Water would be nice, thank you. Ben, please, don't…" Anna started to say, but Ben waved her off.

"Hey, we are the medically weird kids. I get it. I'm gonna worry right now, but once I know you're cool, this never happened." He stood, moving toward the kitchen. "I'll get you some water and tell Mari she doesn't need to call your mom."

Ben left the living room, leaving Nummi and Anna alone. Anna didn't want to look at Nummi, but he was staring at her, saying nothing. After a moment, Anna couldn't take the silence anymore.

Without looking up at him, Anna whispered. "You were in my vision."

"Yes." Nummi replied plainly.

Finally looking back at him, Anna asked. "How?"

"You fell." The old man shrugged. "I tried to grab you, protect your head as you fell, and you took me with you."

"Took you with me?" Anna questioned him. "Took you where? Where did I go?"

Nummi didn't answer at first. He sighed and seemed to weigh his words. Finally, he spoke. "Anna, your spirit is not with your body. It happens sometimes. Spirits will wander away. It goes in dreams, or wanders the earth. Many people have many ideas about where they go. But yours? Yours went somewhere else. Somewhere I have not been in a long time. Your spirit shouldn't be there. It should be…" Nummi shook his head and stopped talking, a perplexed look on his face.

What Nummi was saying sounded absurd to Anna. Spirits wandering away. Wouldn't you just die without your spirit in your body? Anna asked Nummi this and Nummi chuckled.

"Well, I should be happy you are not questioning the existence of a spirit, at least," he replied. "Yes, spirits leave you when you die. They go home, with the gods, or to someplace else. This is another thing most people cannot agree on, but the truth is much simpler than most people know. Some people know that the spirit can wander away from their body while they live, and then come back. It is called many things by many different people. Most people nowadays call it astral projection, but it is all the same. But you, Anna, you are not dead, you are not astral projecting. You are something different."

Anna listened to Nummi talk. The idea of spirits and wandering was new to her, but she knew Nummi's, and by extension Ben and Mari's, beliefs were old. Older than a lot of others on the planet. Ben had told Anna last Halloween that his family had some strange faith that wasn't known too well anymore but was practiced by only a few people around the world. He said it was complicated to explain, but it was older than basically any country on the map and was from a time long before even writing and whatever. Ben had seemed uncomfortable to share more.

At the time, Anna had just wanted to see if Ben wanted to watch scary movies with her instead of going trick-or-treating, and was okay with his statement that their family didn't celebrate Halloween, so

Anna had just let it go. Thinking about it now, though, Anna understood more why Ben had been reluctant to talk about his family's religion. Who wants to be the weird sick kid and the weird religion kid? One weirdness is enough in high school.

While Anna wasn't sure what she believed in, she knew that fake things usually disappeared over time, or got disproven by science. The same was true for religions as it was for anything else, except maybe the timeframe for religions was different than the timeframe for other stuff like medicine. Beliefs didn't last as long as Ben said theirs' had been around unless there was maybe some truth to them. This made Anna inclined to at least accept what Nummi was saying, if for nothing else than the sake of the conversation. He had been in her vision, she reasoned, there must be a purpose for that. As she thought about what Nummi was saying, a questioned formed she wanted to ask but was too scared to.

Nummi could see the question on her face. "No," he said staunchly.

Anna played dumb. "No what?"

"No, I will not tell you where your spirit was." Nummi looked away from her, unwilling to meet her eyes. "You were going to ask it, but no. And no, your spirit is not in Heaven or any other land of the dead. I will tell you someday, maybe, where it is but not now. Knowing a spirit exists and that yours is not where it should be is enough for one day, I think."

Anna sighed in resignation. She recognized the resolution in Nummi's voice enough to realize she wouldn't change his mind. The glint in his eye said he would not tell her more about where her spirit is, no matter what. At least, for now. But that little bit of knowledge only led to more questions for Anna.

"Wait, land of the dead? Doesn't the soul go to the land of the dead, or Heaven or whatever, when you die not the spirit? Spirits are like ghosts, right? Or at least, that's what most people talk about, souls going to Heaven and spirits being ghosts." Anna furrowed her brow, feeling confused.

Nummi smiled, seeing Anna's determination to keep him talking. "There are three parts to people. The body." Nummi patted himself all over and then touched Anna's shoulder again. "Then there is the spirit, the part that is the 'me' when we talk about ourselves." At this, Nummi touched his head then Anna's. "And the final part is the soul. This is the hidden part. The part we keep inside, hidden away from everyone else. The part for the gods and us alone." Nummi touched his chest at his heart, then Anna's as he talked about the soul.

"People use spirit and soul as if they are interchangeable sometimes, but they are not. For humans, the spirit and soul are mostly attached. When alive, the spirit can wander if the person knows how to do that, or is special in ways, but then the soul stays behind. The spirit returns and the two are together again. When someone dies, their spirit and soul go together and leave the body behind. Humans are all like that, whether they are regular or a special type." Nummi took a breath, considering something.

"You have a body, Anna. We all see it. You have a spirit and a soul, too. Your spirit has wandered away from your body, but souls do not wander away, they only leave when you die. When the spirit wanders too long, you get sick. When the soul leaves, you die. The body stops and you die. The body cannot keep going if the soul is gone." Nummi stopped talking as if saying all this should make Anna confident that he was right. His words didn't but Anna decided to just believe him on this, since she was taking his word on everything else too.

After a moment, Nummi started again. "I could find it, if you want."

Anna looked at him. "Find my soul?"

"No," Nummi shook his head. "Find your spirit. It would take some work. I would have to change some things. Do them in a way they aren't usually done, but I believe I could."

Anna opened her mouth to speak, but Ben came back in the room. "Sorry that took so long. Mari was sure she should call your mom. Took everything to convince her not to. Albert is going to drive you home and they both promise not to tell her you fainted again." He handed Anna a glass of water, which she drank if only to cover the odd expression she knew she must have.

After she finished, Anna stood up. Albert had come into the

living room. He was not at all what Anna expected. Fiery red hair and beard, and short but broadly build, with slightly hunching shoulders and a bit of a beer belly, Albert spoke with a distinctly Nordic accent. He was wearing glasses and had on a shirt for some video game. "Ready to truck on?" He asked her.

"Yes, thank you." Anna followed him as he showed her the way to the garage door.

As she walked away, Nummi called after her. "If you want, just tell Ben you say to tell me yes and I will get everything ready." Anna nodded to Nummi that she understood. Now, to go home and talk to Mom. This would be interesting to say the least, she thought.

Bella Part Four

Pain bloomed in the middle of my cheek and I realized I was laying down in the sand. "What the hell did you do that for?"

Gavya laughed. "Well, it worked. You have been unconscious for a week in human time, Bella."

I sat up and started brushing sand from my hands and combing it out of my hair. "A week? No way. You just hit me, just now." Attempting to stand, I looked around for something to brace myself on, and saw a man. An old man with long white hair, tall but stooped from age. He was right there, his hand suddenly on my shoulder. But at the same time, he wasn't. I couldn't feel his hand and, somehow, I could almost see through him. The heat from the sand made him seem distorted, almost like a mirage.

"Who are you?" I asked.

"You shouldn't be here." He replied. "You belong with Anna. You need to come back to her."

I looked at the man, confused. "What? I am Anna. AnnaBella, that's my name. How could I not be with myself?"

The man vanished as quickly as he appeared. In the void where he had been standing, I heard the words echo again. "You shouldn't be here."

Gavya and I stared at each other for a long minute before either of us spoke. "Ok, weird." Gavya finally said. "And B. T. W. who calls you Anna?"

I sighed. "My mom. It was a whole thing. My dad wanted to name me Bella, my mom Anna. They decided to agree to disagree and just smooshed the names together to AnnaBella and each one just called me their preferred nickname."

"Wow." Gavya whistled. "Way to give a child a major identity crisis. Which name do you prefer? I mean, at this point in your life, shouldn't you just choose what to be called?"

I had been set to argue with Gavya that my name issue had never really been a problem for me, but her question caught me off guard. Which name did I prefer? Anna or Bella? Wouldn't choosing one be the same as choosing between Mom and Dad? Could I do that? No.

That is the same choice the speaker gave me and I couldn't choose then. Why would I be able to choose now? But there is a third option. Going for the whole thing and choosing AnnaBella. That makes me not choose between Mom and Dad. But that is such a mouthful. AnnaBella. Anna. Bella. Gods of all the infinite foreverness, what the ever-loving crap! Gavya wants me to choose my name now. Right now. Who I am. Who I want to be. Can I just pick something else entirely? Like Sue. Sue is a good name. An easy name. No nicknames needed there. No arguing over this or that. Sue isn't short for anything. Well, maybe short for Susan. So not Sue. What about…

Gavya grabbed my arm and shook me gently, pulling me out of my existential crisis. "Like I said, identity crisis from birth, yeah?" She stopped shaking me. "Listen, no one, especially not me, is asking you to figure out that," Gavya waved her arms, gesturing up and down my body, "that mess right now. Just tuck it away in the back of your brain. Food for thought for later. Later. Like when we aren't fleeing from authorities and sitting in the sand in a hot desert with you slowly sunburning to death. For now, let's think about finding shelter."

At the mention of sunburns, I looked at myself. Really looked at myself. Gavya said I had been laying out there in the sand for a week. And ouch, my skin was red, really red. There were a few spots, like in the creases of my elbows, where water blisters had started to form. Looking around, I saw that Gavya had attempted to use her saree to create a shelter of sorts over me, but the wind had just tossed the fabric around. I could see that Gavya would have gotten frustrated with repositioning it a million times and given up. She had just let the wind toss the fabric around and had left it sitting where it lay in the sand, half buried.

Around her, were all the documents we had 'borrowed' from the Annex. Some of them were laid flat, bottles of water from the bag holding them down, obviously drying from being stuffed in sweat-soaked waistbands and bras. Others were open to specific pages, in piles, as if she had been comparing notes. Apparently, Gavya had not been wasting her time while I was unconscious.

"Where do we go then?" I asked. "We can't go back into Taikarlu. The Avenging Women would still be after us, wouldn't they? And the Waste is just more of the same for who knows how far."

Gavya held up one finger. "I have a thought on that." She started pulling books and rolls and papers towards her. "There used to be a bunch of fantastical creatures around Taikarlu. Humans know some of them. Unicorns and djinns and sprites and whatever. Humans call them mythological because they disappeared during the flood, so they haven't seen them in forever and forgot they used to be real. But we, here, know they were. Some gods think they all died in the flood but that doesn't make sense. If they died, where are the corpses? They could be hiding in the Wastes. Trapped here, maybe even. Same way most people in Taikarlu get turned around in the Wastes and end up back where they came from, maybe the beasties get turned around so they can't leave. If they are, they must have access to food and water. Contrary to popular human opinion, most of the mythological beasties still need to eat and drink like normal. Coordinators and gods? No. Beasties? Yes."

Gavya's thought process made sense to me. "So, you are suggesting that somewhere in the unexplored vastness of the Wastes, there are probably some oases where the mythological beasts are safe from the prying eyes of humans and gods. That would make a wonderful hideout for a spirit with a human body that has disappeared and a coordinator on the run from the Avenging Women. But how do we find one?" I looked around, out into the desert, in every direction except back towards the Hills. There was no sign of vegetation or life anywhere.

Gavya, who had been sitting up straight and tall, using her authoritative, I run the Annex voice and posture, deflated. "That I don't know. Do we just pick a way and guess? Hope we don't end up walking back to Taikarlu?"

"That could be potentially catastrophic." I replied, then started picking up handfuls of sand and dumping them, thinking. I began wishing that the sand could speak, because then I could just compel the sand to tell me where safety was.

Wait a minute… I have forced things to tell me the truth without being able to speak to them before. Heck, I forced a lie from something that wasn't even sentient before. In the Trials, I got the bull to tell me what it wanted, and I made the clock lie. Maybe I could convince the sand to tell me where water is.

"Gavya," I said slowly, "watch my back for a minute. I am gonna try to do something a little odd. Don't interrupt me, I have messed up big doing this before."

Gavya looked at me crossways. "Yeah, the clock thing. We all know about that. What are you planning, Bella?"

"Just a little compulsion of inanimate objects again." I replied evasively. "I promise, not time. Never again will I do time."

Gavya kept looking at me as if she thought I would blow up the world, but put up her hands in resignation. She wouldn't interfere. I reached down and grabbed a handful of sand, holding it tightly in a fist. Closing my eyes, I looked deep inside for that warm over ice feeling. Finding it had been so easy in the courtroom when I was compelling dead humans to give me the real details about their actions in life. But out here, in the wilds of the Wastes, everything felt so far away from me. My arm burned. My sunburnt skin felt tight. My mind found a million distractions. My brain told me not to use the Heka or the Avenging Women would know where I am. It told me my Heka won't work on sand, what am I thinking?

I opened my eyes and took a breath. This will work, I told myself. It has to work. Otherwise, I die. Well, maybe I die. I wasn't really clear what would happen to me. But Gavya was stuck. If I did not find a way to get back to my body, prove the gods had broken every rule ever in keeping me from it, she would never be free to go home. She sacrificed her immortal life for me. And I can't do anything to help her if I just give up and sit in the middle of a desert in the blistering sun. I needed to do this. I needed to believe this will work.

I closed my eyes again, holding the sand. Lead me to water, I thought. There it was, the ice and heat. Faint, but there. I latched onto that tiny feeling deep inside me and thought again. Lead me to water. To safety. My arm tingled.

The ever-present wind suddenly stopped. Somewhere in front of me, Gavya whistled in awe. I ignored her. Tell me the truth, I pushed. Where is water? Where is safety?

The sand in my hand shifted. I had my fist balled up tightly and all the excess sand had already fell away. I could feel what was left moving, though. Each grain seemed to quivering. I opened my hand, palm up, to let the sand do what it wanted.

It didn't just fall. I would have felt it fall to the ground around me, but it didn't. The wind was still. My hair had stopped blowing around my face, and the sweat on my brow was not being dried before it could cool me. But the sand was blowing out of my hand.

Gavya spoke again. "What in the world?" I opened my eyes. The sand in my hand was blowing away in a straight line. Grain by grain, the sand made a straight line to the north.

I started to speak but Gavya interrupted me. "No. Don't break your concentration. Whatever you are doing, keep doing it." My handful of sand was getting empty, so Gavya stood, scooped up a pile of sand and added it to my hand. Then she began quickly gathering everything. She didn't even bother wrapping her saree around her, but just slung the material over one shoulder. Books and papers got crammed into the bag haphazardly.

When everything was collected, Gavya came over to me and offered me an arm. With my empty hand, I grabbed onto her and stood, never breaking my concentration. Tell me the truth. Where is water?   Where   is   safety?
Gavya and I started walking, following the particles of sand that flew out of my hand and soared north in a straight line, racing each other to go somewhere. Every once in a while, my hand would start to get empty. The line of grains of sand leading the way would start to thin.

Each time, Gavya stopped and picked up a new pile of sand and put it in my palm. The line would thicken again and we continued on our way.

We walked for what felt like hours like this, due north. Mile after mile of nothing but waves of sand and silence. Several times, Gavya would stop even though the trail of sand wasn't thin. These times, she dug in the bag and produced a bottle of water, tipping it near my lips so I could drink without breaking my concentration.

After several times of reloading my handful of sand and making me drink, Gavya told me, "Don't think about it, but this is the last bottle of water. Don't worry, just drink." She opened the bottle and dumped it into my mouth, like a mama bird feeding her baby. "Keep concentrating on the path." I kept thinking about the path. Tell me the truth. Where is water? Where is safety?

The trail of sand always dropped immediately as Gavya and I passed it. Behind us, the wind was blowing as normal, wiping away our footprints. The sand was doing as asked and providing safety for our journey. No one could follow us, if anyone was trying to. But I noticed none of this. Nor did I notice when Gavya gasped and started running ahead of me. I just kept a firm mental hand on my ice and heat. It felt slippery, like if I didn't concentrate all of me on It, It would run away and hide again. I kept thinking over and over again, "Tell me the truth. Where is water? Where is safety?" So, I was surprised when my footsteps hit firm land instead of the shifting ground and I saw my hand had become empty of sand.

I finally looked up. There was grass and trees. The air smelled fresh and cool and I could hear water bubbling up from somewhere. We had found an oasis. Just a dense patch of growth out in the middle of the desert. I hadn't come out of my trance until we were deep within the oasis. I walked back the way we had come while I was entranced to find the edge of the oasis. It wasn't a distinct edge like in movies, but instead a gradual fading. The grass was slowly replaced by sand and the trees shrunk and twisted until they disappeared altogether.

"Bella!" I heard Gavya calling me from somewhere deep in the oasis. Following the sound of her voice, I found her at the edge of a small pond. A few feet away from one edge of the pond was a cavern carved out of a rocky outcropping. The water that formed the pond was trickling out of the cavern in a tiny rivulet that ran to the pond. "Fresh water." She pointed at the pond. "Drink, bathe, refresh your almost human body." The look of relief on her face told me how worried Gavya had actually become over me.

My mind had still been in a haze from concentrating on the compulsion so long. But all that went away as soon as I jumped into the pond. The water was cold! It felt amazing. My skin, still so sunburned, tightened painfully at the sudden temperature shift, but I didn't care. I dunked my head under the water and felt all of the stress just melt away.

"We could stay here for a long time," Gavya was telling me while I soaked in the coolness of the water and drank until I thought I would burst. "Look there." She pointed over at a bush. "Raspberries. And there, some sort of rodent. Meat. This oasis is alive with food and fresh water. I bet there is a natural underground spring in that cavern. We could probably find a corner out of the way to make a safe place to sleep and get out of the sun."

Gavya said all of this while walking around. She went back to the bags and got the fabric of her saree. Wrapping it back around her waist, she smiled. "Your sand told us where safety was. It brought us straight here, to this oasis. Your power, it's amazing." There was a tinge of awe in Gavya's voice.

To hide from her sudden accolades over what I just forced to work because I needed it to, I dunked under the water and swam for a bit. Opening my eyes, I saw fish. Small ones but obviously they had never seen people before. They swam right up to me, curious. I could catch them and eat them. Like Gavya said, so much food potential here.

We would have to be careful though. Not get greedy. I would hate to stay here for a while and just overindulge and destroy the ecology. Enough humans are doing that on earth, I didn't need to become one of them in Taikarlu, or wherever we technically were.

I decided to finally come up and hope Gavya had moved on from her praises. When I broke the water's surface, I saw her. Gavya's back was to me and she was looking away into the trees. Slowly, regretfully, I climbed out of the pond and walked towards her. I didn't bother drying off. While the temperature in the oasis was much cooler than it had been in the Wastes, it was still very warm and my wet clothes and hair felt good.

I came over and stood beside Gavya, looking the same direction she was. "Did you see that?" Gavya pointed into a clump of trees about twenty feet away. I looked where she was pointing and saw nothing.

"There was something there." Gavya's voice faded away. She seemed not to be trusting her own eyes.

I put my arm around her shoulder. "Come on, don't worry about it. Let's go explore the cave and see if there is a spot we can make our temporary home." I pulled Gavya, making her walk with me. She looked back at the clump of trees, then looked away, and back one more time.

"I really thought," she began, then shook her head. "Never mind. It has been a really long day. Or week, month, however long it has been. Let's just get comfortable. I am sure we are safe here. You asked the sand for safety with your Heka. I am sure that is exactly what they provided."

Gavya and I walked to the cave, leaving our belongings on the grass by the pond. We could come back for them if we found a good spot. The mouth of the cave was just tall enough for me, but Gavya, an inch or so taller than me, had to duck so she didn't hit her head. Inside the mouth of the cave, the light disappeared quickly. I squinted, trying to force my eyes to adjust to the change. As soon as they did, I looked around. The mouth of the cave was close, Gavya and I just barely had space to stand side by side. But only a few feet in, the walls widened, making a large spacious area. Through the center of the space, a small trickle of water had obviously been flowing for some time. A trough had been cut through the stone only as wide as the palm of my hand, but inside it, the water filled the space, flowing quickly out the mouth and into the pond.

Gavya began walking around the edge, following the walls in the open space. I chose to follow the water, tracing it back to hopefully find its source. The open space continued back for a while, but then narrowed. There was a tunnel, about as wide as the mouth of the cave at the back wall. The channel of water went through the tunnel, so I kept following it. Slowly, the small amount of light from the mouth of the cave got dimmer and dimmer until I could not see my way anymore. I stopped and peered down into the darkness. It could have been another two feet or a hundred mile until the source of the water and I would never know. Regretfully, I turned around and walked back to Gavya. We would have to find a light source if we wanted to explore deeper.

While I had been exploring, apparently Gavya had decided the left side of the open space just inside the mouth of the cave was the perfect spot to make our home. She had moved most of the supplies to the front left corner and seemed to be trying to find some organization system for the texts that kept them dry but available.

"We need a light to go far enough back in the cave to find the natural spring." I told Gavya.

Gavya just shrugged in response and kept sorting out our supplies. "Do you want me to find a way to make you a bed? I bet we could find some nice soft moss and leaves to make a bed."

So, that's a no on exploring deeper, I thought questioningly. Glancing at Gavya, I saw a slight furrow to her brow. She was still worrying about that whatever it was in the clump of trees. She needed to stop worrying. I had to make her stop worrying. I told the sand to lead us to safety and it led us here. We could either trust the sand or not trust it. I voted for trusting it, even if that did mean accepting that I must have some sort of power that went beyond what Dad gave me and made inanimate objects compellable more than just to tell the truth. And either way, if we weren't safe here and the sand was wrong or we just hallucinated all of this, we still had no other options. Might as well go for positive instead worrying when there is literally nothing more we could do.

"Yeah, a bed might be nice." I told Gavya. "I can go start foraging if you want to stay here and keep working."

Gavya finally stopped working and looked at me. "Maybe," she started but then stopped. Trying again, she said "Are you sure you should be walking around on your own?"

Trying to play it all off to alleviate her fears of the maybe thing out in the unknown of the oasis, I rolled my eyes. "Gavya, there is nothing out there, and if there is, who cares? If it hasn't bugged us yet, I don't think it will."

"No, no, no." Gavya shook her head. "My concern was not that, but thanks for reminding me about another worry. I was more worried that you kinda sorta tend to pass out occasionally with no warning and have visions. Plus, that whole thing with the disappearing old man. I mean, maybe I should keep an eye on you in case he comes back and actually tries something to make you not be here anymore."

Oh yeah, that. I forgot about that. As much as I hated to admit it, Gavya probably had a good point. I did not however get a chance to tell her that because, as if manifested from her comment, the old man was standing behind her.

"Um, Gavya," I started. "Speaking of the devil, look behind you."

Gavya turned and gasped. The old man was looking around, as if confused where he was. "You moved." He seemed surprised.

I stuttered in response. "Uh, yeah. I can do that. We moved somewhere safe."

"This is not safe." The old man sounded resolute, almost angry. "Safe is with your body. Safe is not here. Where is here?"

Gavya started to say something, but I stopped her. "Before we start answering your questions, maybe you should answer a few of ours first. Who are you? Why are you here? How are you here? Why do you look like an apparition?"

"The impatience of youth." The old man chuckled. "My name is not important. You, the other you, Anna, calls me Nummi. That is the name I was called a long time ago and the name Ben calls me. Ben introduced Anna to me. You, this you, may call me Nummi as well. I was first brought here by Anna accidentally when she collapsed and had a vision of you. I was touching her and she brought me with her."

The old man held up his hands, holding them wide as he explained. "You are Anna's spirit. You need to come home. I put myself in a trance, a spiritual one, to allow my own spirit to find you and determine why you are separated from Anna, from your body. Something has gone very wrong here. As for how I look, I have no idea how you perceive me, but you look hollow to me. Transparent, so to speak. This may be how we perceive each other but see ourselves as whole because I am only half here. I have tied a spiritual rope to myself before letting me wander from the human realms so I will not get lost too. I have never been here before or found wandering spirits here before so I do not wish to become stuck here somehow as well. Does this answer all your questions, young one?"

"Um, yeah. That about covers it. I think." I told the man. "We are in Taikarlu, the land of the gods. Or really, in the Wastes outside Taikarlu. Separating Taikarlu?" I looked confusedly at Gavya, hoping for clarification. She just shrugged, so I continued. "I am called Bella here, the other half of my name. I did not wander from my body, but came to Taikarlu with my father. He is from here, not human. The gods tricked me because I was an unauthorized child and now, I have a ward in my arm preventing me from going back to humans. Um, it's a whole thing. Long story and all that."

"A ward?" Nummi rubbed his forehead, as if confused.

I held up my right arm to show him the scar. "Yeah. Wait, you said you know my body? Like my human body? And people are calling her Anna? Is she with my mom? And Ben is there? The same Ben from my Trials or a different Ben? Ben is a common name, actually. If it is the same Ben, how is Ben there? I thought he was only in the Trials, a computerized projection or something. Wait, that's not important right now. What is important is that my body is walking around and talking to people. What does she, I mean me, I mean the Anna part of me think happened? What does my mom think happened while I was with Dad all summer?"

Nummi held up his hands. "Young one with so many questions. Please, there is not time. You are Warded by the gods to stay here, in their lands? Your body is on earth, with your mother. You and her believe that your father died in a car accident. She has no memory of him as being from these lands. The gods did this to you? This problem goes deeper than even I thought."

Nummi and I stared at each other. Gavya, her mouth hanging

open, kept looking back and forth at him and then me. The old man seemed to be thinking while I just sat dumbfounded. My human body was walking around, talking, thinking Dad was just a regular guy who was dead. Not remembering any of this? Not remembering the Trials or the gods or any of this?

"Am I sick?" I asked. "Gavya and I had found that book that said there were tribes of people who believed spirits could wander, but if gone too long, the body would get sick. Is Anna sick, I mean?"

"Yes, very." Nummi nodded, rubbing his chin. "I must go. I must tell the others. The gods have done something very wrong here, if they did this to you. To the two parts of you. We knew something was wrong, but I never thought this. We need to figure out what they did and how to fix it. Will you stay here? Where I can find you again easily?"

I nodded yes. I was too stunned to speak. I watched as the apparition of Nummi went to a wall of the cave and did something to it. To me, it looked like he was just waving his arms around, but he spoke again.

"I have drawn a symbol on this wall to lead me back here. Do not wash it away. I will return." At this, Nummi vanished. In the empty space he left behind, the word "return" echoed.

Gavya and I just stared at one another. This seemed to be happening often, us ending up confused and staring at each other. Speechless, I looked from her to the empty wall where Nummi had apparently drawn something we couldn't see. My brain tried to form coherent thoughts but all that came out was, "My body is walking around calling itself Anna on earth while I am walking around calling myself Bella up here."

Gavya nodded. So, I did say that out loud. I wasn't sure. My mind was still reeling when she finally responded. "Told you. Identity crisis. You just had to go being all extra and make yourself literally split in two to have it." Gavya chose sarcastic teasing while I opted for shocked confusion, apparently.

Her teasing pulled me out of my stupor. I snorted, holding back laughter. Gavya looked away from me and her shoulders started shaking. Eventually, she couldn't hold back, and I heard her laughing.

I smiled, biting my lip, but everything was just too much. Before I realized what was happening, Gavya and I were laughing so hard we were crying, holding on to each other, and falling on the cavern floor.

Soon, we were wheezing. "Oh man." I squeezed out. "Oof, wow."

"Yeah," Gavya said breathlessly. She sat up and pulled her disheveled outfit straight, trying to gather her composure. "Well, we did learn a few very important things from that old man."

"Nummi," I corrected, copying her change toward seriousness. "He said to call him Nummi."

"Nummi," she repeated. "Yes. Ok, well, we know a few things from him. One, you are absolutely a spirit separated from your body. Your body, Anna, is walking around with the humans having no bloody idea that you are, you both are, the child of a coordinator and a human who have the power to be a god."

"Two," I held up two fingers, "there is at least one person who knows how to go between the two of us, from Anna to me and back again. That means Anna and I can communicate if we need to. Not that I would know how to get Nummi here if I needed him, or what I might need to tell Anna that Nummi isn't probably telling her right now. Like that I am here, I am stuck here, and have no idea how to get back together as one with her."

Gavya raised three fingers. "Three, your visions are not just visions. You literally are connecting with Anna. And she with you. He didn't say so, but I assume if you are passing out and having visions of what she is experiencing, she would be doing the same."

"And four," I added, "there is at least someone who has some idea of wandering spirits disconnected from their bodies who is attempting to come up with a plan to fix this mess. Maybe more than just one somebody, Nummi said he had to tell the others. I wonder what others? And how do they, or at least he, know about Taikarlu? I hate questions I can't answer. It feels like a test, like high school all over again. I guess all we can do is wait for Nummi to come back. He said he would. The question becomes then, what do we do while we wait for him?"

"Survive?" Gavya shrugged. "Get comfortable? Human time

and Taikarlu time are skewed from each other, as we well know. Let's just wait and see if old Nummi comes back and tells us what to do next. Until then, you hungry?"

I thought about that for a second then realized I was famished. I grabbed Gavya's arm with both hands. "Oh gods, yes! Feed me, please, Gavya!"

Anna Part Three

Anna slammed her bookbag down on the lab bench. She was completely over school today, but still had to finish biology class yet. At least Ben would be in class today. He had been out for the last two days because of an appointment with the plastic surgeon. One of his burns on his shoulder had been given him some trouble, making it hard to lift his arm completely, and his dermatologist suggested reconstructive surgery might help. The surgeon the dermatologist had recommended was at a university hospital down state, hours away, and his sister and he made an overnight trip of the appointment.

As Anna plopped down on her stool, Ben came up behind her. "Howdy."

"Hey," she said, turning around to face him. "How'd it go with the plastic surgeon?"

Ben shrugged, "Eh. He wants me to do some PT before they go poking around with a scalpel but that would mean missing even more school than I already do. No thanks. I can just google some stuff and try it at home."

Anna knew she should try to tell him that wasn't the best of ideas. Ben could do worse damage trying to do it without professional help or injure something else. But she knew from past conversations that Ben would only scoff and be more determined to go his own way, so she left it alone.

Ben was still talking anyway, so Anna turned off those worrying thoughts and listened. "So, you may think this is super weird and I told him he was nuts to make me pass this message on when it may make absolutely no sense to you, but whatever. Nummi said to tell you that he saw your spirit Bella, he talked to her, and she is stuck in the land of the gods. If you want to fix it, and connect your spirit and body back together, we need to do it fast because the gods trapped her there and if they find out what we are up to, they will probably get super angry and find a way to stop it."

Ben was speaking really fast, but he kept going. "All of this may make absolutely no sense to you because I know there is a whole bunch of stuff we haven't told you yet and you would have to just take a lot of this on faith that we aren't crazy. But anyway, you are supposed to tell me yes or no. Do you want to do this? Yes or no? Or do you think we just lost it?"

"Will it hurt?" I asked.

Ben sighed. "See, I knew you needed more than just the basics. No, it won't hurt. You basically will go to sleep for a little bit. Your spirit side will do most of the work."

Anna sat back, a little shocked. Nummi found her spirit and it is calling itself Bella? In the land of the gods? There is such a place? Ben was looking at Anna expectantly. She felt pressured to respond. Oh, what the hell, she thought.

"Yes," Anna replied.

"What?" Ben seemed confused.

Anna sighed, had the chance to back out, thought about it but didn't. "Tell Nummi I said yes."

Ben pulled out the stool next to Anna and sat down. Anna turned on her stool, following his path so she could look at him. "You understood all of that?" He gave her a quizzical look, still confused.

"Yeah, I did," she breathed. "Well, kind of. Actually, not much of it. I have a bunch of questions. But I understood enough. Tell Nummi I said yes, just let me know when and where." I gotta tell Mom, she thought to herself.

Ben seemed surprised at Anna's answer. "I swear, we will explain everything better. Nummi thinks that telling you too much right now will weird you out or something. But thank you for trusting him."

Ben seemed as if he wanted to say something more, but the teacher started talking, so he said no more about it. But Anna couldn't be distracted. She did not hear a word Ms. Eberrake said the whole class period. Instead, she was too busy worrying about what reconnecting a lost spirit with its body entailed and how bad the fallout could be if the gods (gods are real and there's more than one?) were the ones who disconnected them. She spent the rest of class, and the entire walk home, lost in the clouds of thought. Ben, noticing her distraction, left her alone with her thoughts.

Ben walked beside Anna the whole way home, even though his house was the opposite way. He just escorted her, neither of them saying a word. He seemed to be anxious, as if Anna would turn to him at any minute and think he was a freak or mental and run away. When they arrived at Anna's house, he watched as she climbed the steps to the house and stopped with her hand on the doorknob. Anna did not even notice Ben watching her, then turning away, shaking his head to walk the rest of the way to his house alone.

Anna's hand sat on the knob of the front door for several minutes. She knew her mom was home because the gray hatchback was sitting in the driveway. What do I say to her? Anna thought. How do I explain to her everything that Nummi told me? How do I make it make sense, get her to be okay with me doing something different, something that medicine wouldn't understand or probably approve of, to try to fix what all the doctors say isn't fixable? Something from a culture neither of us know anything about?

Sighing, Anna decided to just wing it. What to say would come to her, she hoped. Opening the door, Anna entered the living room and saw Mom gracefully moving around the living room, watering her plants and humming a tune. Oh, good, Anna thought, she's in a good mood.

"Hey Mom," Anna tried to force her voice to be casual.

Mom looked up from the spider plant she had been examining for mites or other parasites. "Oh, hey baby. How was school?"

Anna shrugged. "It was school." Still attempting to keep a forced nonchalant attitude, Anna continued. "Um, Mom. I was wondering. Can we talk for a minute? I have a question."

Mom set down the watering can next to the spider plant and moved to sit on the couch. "Of course, Anna. What's on your mind?"

Anna sat on the loveseat and rubbed her knees. Her hands were sweating, but she didn't want Mom to know. "So, this, um, may seem like a weird question, but…" Anna paused, telling her brain to kick in with some genius idea any second now. She looked around the living room, her eyes falling on the map of the world. The whole map was black and white outlines of every country, but some of the lines had marker on them and other spots were colored in. The marker lines were dry erase that Anna's mother had wrote on the map to indicate where borders of countries had changed since the map was made and the permanent coloring was where Mom and Anna had visited. Blue countries marked where Mom had traveled to alone, red for Anna, and purple if they had gone together. The map had a lot of areas in blue, a few in purple and really only part of the United States in red. Anna's brain finally figured out an idea.

Anna looked back to her mother, who seemed to be waiting patiently. "You know how you have been to a lot of places and seen a lot of cultures that do things really differently than we do here?"

Mom nodded, curling her legs under her in an attempt to get more comfortable in her seat. "Oh yeah," she smiled, "that is one of the best parts of my job. Going to all those places, learning new cultures, trying new foods. Or well, it was before the accident. It was so much fun, I miss it."

"Yeah." Anna took a deep breath. "Well, I was wondering. Did you ever stop to wonder if those cultures might be doing things right and we do things wrong?"

Mom sighed and shook her head. "Oh, Anna, there is no right or wrong with that stuff. I mean, well, yeah there is some wrong. Like when a culture denies a person basic human rights because of something they can't control, like being a girl or gay or some other religion than the main one practiced there. That's wrong and that's what I do. I come in and try to help people fix those wrongs. But, in general, how one culture decides to do things versus another is not a right or wrong issue, but just a different issue. Like what type of houses they live in, or what clothes they wear, or food they eat, that type of stuff isn't wrong or right, just different."

"What about how they practice medicine?" Anna asked.

Mom thought for a moment before answering. "I guess, in a way, that too. As long as the people, all the people, have access to medicine and life-saving technology when they need it, every culture is going to practice medicine differently. I have gone places and seen some cultures that have shamans and medicine men who treat spiritual diseases the culture believes in and still be happy to have their children vaccinated against small pox and be excited to have procedures to fix medical ailments."

Mom shifted in her seat, tipping her head to the side, remembering as she talked. "Most of the time I was there for other reasons, like helping the people protect their rights to continue to live the way they wanted without the governments forcing them to change, but sometimes doctors went too to help make sure the communities still received fair access to medicine. I remember one time a shaman for this small tribe was so happy when the doctors I was traveling with diagnosed one of the children with diabetes and were able to treat the boy, because he had never heard of it and his spiritual healing wasn't working. We worked together with the shaman. He did the spiritual side, and the doctors did the medical side. It was wonderful and so cool to watch. I felt really privileged to be included in that when it had nothing to do with the law side of stuff."

Anna knew this was starting to get to the root of what she wanted and pushed her mom further into that line of thinking. "So, you believe in the spiritual issues? You think that sometimes things can be spirit illness not physical illnesses?"

"Um, I don't know. I think…" Mom paused, not saying anything for a moment. Anna could tell Mom was thinking before speaking and gave her the time to process what to say, but that pause made Anna nervous. Everything hinged on what Mom said next.

Finally, Mom continued. "I think that I wouldn't discount the spiritual side of thing. Do I think it is totally real? I'm not sure. But what I do know is that the people treated by these shamans and the like sometimes do feel better when nothing else has worked. I know that the emotional, cultural side to treating medical ailments is a necessary part of that work. The doctors I have traveled with told me that if someone believes there is a spiritual illness, that even if there is a known medical illness there that is totally treated and cured, that person will not get better until the spiritual work is done too. Does that make sense?"

"Yeah, yeah," Anna responded. Mom's response did not give her a lot of encouragement, but Anna hoped it meant her mom would be at least open-minded about the whole idea. "Have you ever, I dunno, looked into the cultural beliefs of people from a long time ago? Ones that almost no one practices anymore?"

Mom responded like she still thought Anna was just curious rather than that there was a point to the conversation. "Sure, honey. There are so many different cultures, even ones right here in our own back yard, that have been practiced for a long time. It's sad, they all kinda get lumped in as one group, but there are so many different beliefs and cultures and practices. I don't know a lot about them but have worked with one or two groups here and there. And I know there are a lot of ancient beliefs that aren't followed anymore, and some that are almost extinct except in small pockets."

Mom had a small shy smile, the smile she got when she started talking about things she wished she knew more about. "I studied law in school, not sociology or anthropology, so I don't know much about them. Sometimes I wish I had minored in sociology or something during my bachelor's degree instead of philosophy. It is so cool and would help me in my job so much. But I have worked with enough sociologists to know that there are too many beliefs for one person to ever know about all of them. Are you interested in learning more about any one in specific?"

"Well, that's the thing, Mom." Anna took a deep breath and decided to plunge right in. She spoke in a rush, hoping she said everything right and in a way Mom would understand. "So, my friend Ben is from one of those cultures that are ancient and not many people follow anymore. His grandpa, Nummi, I think used to be like one of those shaman or wise men for their culture that you were talking about and when I went over to Ben's house to work on that project with him, I met Nummi and he is really cool and he said that he could tell that all this stuff making me sick, like in his culture they would say that it is because my spirit is separated from my body and that he knows how to fix it and it would be a ceremony he could do to fix it and it wouldn't hurt or anything, I would just kind of feel like I am asleep, and you could be there too if you wanted and since the doctors can't figure anything out, I figured what the hell, why not give this a shot and Ben told me that Nummi said he is ready now and can do it whenever we want and if you are ok with it, I wanna do it and just see what happens."

Anna stopped to catch her breath. She was afraid to look at her mom. Instead, she looked down, picking at a frayed corner in the holes in the knees of her jeans. When Mom didn't say anything, Anna glanced up at her.

Mom's face was blank. Anna expected her mother to look angry, or at least very displeased. But she wasn't. Her mother spoke carefully. "Tell me again, Anna. Slowly, this time please."

Anna took a breath and let it go, blowing it out through pursed lips to calm herself. "Ben's grandpa knows a ceremony that will supposedly help all the issues I have been having that the doctors can't understand. He thinks it is a spiritual illness, not a physical one. I want to try it. If he is wrong, it doesn't hurt anything. But what if he is right?"

"How much?" Mom asked.

Anna looked at her mother, confused. "How much what?"

Mom continued having a blank face Anna couldn't read. "How much is Ben's grandfather going to charge us to do the ceremony?"

"Wha.. I.. Uh.." Anna stumbled. This was not how she thought her mother would respond. "Nothing. He isn't charging us anything."

Mom's face changed from blank to surprised and back to blank again. This time, the blank was masking some other feeling Anna couldn't quite put her finger on. Mom looked away from Anna, not looking at anything in specific but just staring off.

"Mom?" Anna said tentatively.

"I want to talk to him." Mom stood up and began gathering her things. She put her shoes on and her coat, then grabbed the keys and her purse from beside the front door.

Anna watched, then jumped up to follow her mother. "Oh, like right now? Um, ok."

Anna followed her mother to the car and got in the passenger seat. Mom got in the driver's side and they drove to Ben's house together. It was a short drive, and Anna tried for the first moment or two to engage Mom in conversation. Mom kept her responses terse, saying only "Hm," or "Uh-huh," but never any actual words. Anna eventually gave up trying to talk and the two drove the rest of the few minutes in silence.

When Mom pulled into Ben's driveway, she got out and headed for the front door without waiting to see if Anna was following. Mom knocked on the door while Anna was still walking up the front steps.

Ben answered the door after only a few seconds, "Yes?" he said, then peered around Mom and saw Anna, "Oh, hey Anna. What's up?"

"My mom wants to talk to Nummi." Anna replied, huffing a little from trying to keep up with Mom.

Ben furrowed his brow quizzically and then shrugged, opening the door wide to let them both in. He showed Mom up the stairs and gestured towards the living room couch, where Nummi was watching a cooking show with subtitles on. Mom walked in the door and over to where Ben indicated.

"Are you Nummi?" she asked the older man.

Nummi looked away from the television and slowly stood. "You must be Anna's mom," he replied. "Yes, I am Ben's grandfather. The children call me Nummi. You may as well. I have been expecting you would want to talk with me." Nummi put out his hand to shake Mom's.

Mom took the proffered hand, quickly shaking it then letting go. "My name is Julia. Nice to meet you, Nummi. What is this my daughter is talking about a spirit healing ceremony?"

Nummi nodded, and then gestured to the other couch. "Yes, yes. I can tell you all about it. Please have a seat, Julia."

Ben and Anna watched this from the top of the stairs. Ben looked at Anna and cocked his head to one side, pointing towards the kitchen with his chin. "Peanut butter cookies? This may take a bit, I think."

Anna nodded in agreement and the two left the adults talking, and headed into the kitchen. They sat for almost a half an hour, munching on cookies, and talked about the gossip at school while they waited.

"No, seriously. Mr. Cannon is the worst. I hate gym class." Ben was saying when Mari poked her head into the kitchen.

"Hey, Anna," Mari interrupted them. "Your mom wants you."

Anna looked at Ben and moaned under her breath. "Better go see how bad this will be."

Ben smiled. "Hey, maybe she will be cool about it. Whatever 'it' is."

Anna walked back to the living room and Ben followed. Mom was standing up in the center of the room with Nummi, her arms crossed over her chest, shifting her weight from one foot to another. The two were still talking in low voices, but Mom's face wasn't blank anymore. Instead, she looked almost reluctantly hopeful.

Mom noticed Anna come in and smiled at her, gesturing for Anna to join them. "Anna," she said, "Nummi and I have talked."

"And?" Anna tried to be hopeful.

"Your mother is willing to let me help you if I can." Nummi replied. "Go now, and have some good food." Anna opened her mouth to speak but Nummi put up a hand to stop her. "Not just cookies. A good meal. Your favorite, if you can. Something that reminds you of your father, I think would be best. Come back tonight after you are full. Between now and then, focus on yourself. The yourself that you think of as you. Immerse yourself in thoughts about what you think makes you, you. Come back to me in peace and calm, with your mind full of all the things that you love."

"Is this part of the ceremony?" Anna asked.

"Not really. But it helps. At least, I am hoping it will. Remember, you are different than a normal walking spirit. You are not dreaming, and your spirit isn't just lost." Nummi paused, then continued, a slight chuckle in his voice. "In either case, are you going to complain that your mother has to buy you your favorite foods for dinner?"

Anna, knowing exactly what she would ask for to eat, smiled. "No. No, I won't." She and Mom turned and left the house, got in the car and drove straight to Yasmeen's Takeout. Anna had not been there since her father died, but it was the best food she could think of because it reminded her of him.

Mom still wasn't talking much, but Anna thought that was okay since it gave her time to do as Nummi said. She focused all her thoughts on the things she thought made her unique. She thought of her dad a lot, and the fun times she had with him. She thought of traveling with her mom, and all the things she did before the car accident. She thought of Ben and talking with him, laughing and doing schoolwork. In her mind, Anna realized that, even though she was sad that she lost her dad, she was glad that the accident helped her find a friend in Ben. Her life was so different than she thought it would be, so different than she had been imagining at the beginning of last summer, but it was not all bad. She focused on the good and, before she knew it, they were driving back to Ben's house, with Anna happy and contented in herself and her stomach full, with leftovers in the backseat.

In the short two hours they had been gone, Ben's living room had been completely transformed. The furniture was all pushed out of the way and the curtains had been pulled tightly shut. The television was off and the room smelled faintly spicy, but not like cooking. In the middle of the now open floor space, there were pillows covered by blankets, forming a small cot.

Nummi took Anna by the hand and led her to the cot. "Julia, please, make yourself comfortable anywhere. Anna, take off your shoes and lie down here comfortably."

Anna did as instructed, lying down on the small cot on the floor on her back. She folded her arms over her chest out of nervous habit, but Nummi pulled her hands apart to lay her arms at her sides. When she had wiggled into a comfortable position, Nummi continued talking.

"Anna, close your eyes and breathe in and out slowing while I count. Your mother is right here beside you. You will be safe with her watching." Anna closed her eyes, and did as Nummi said, taking a deep breath. As she began to exhale, Nummi started counting, "1, 2, 3, 4…" all the way to ten. Then he started again at one.

Anna matched her breathing to his counting and felt herself relax. Here goes nothing, she thought.

Bella Part Five

I let myself go slack and floated in the water. For the gods only know how long, Gavya and I had been staying in the oasis, waiting for a reappearance of the apparition named Nummi. In a place where the sun never set, the weather never changed, and with nothing we had to do, it was hard to keep track of time. Every so often, I would get hungry or thirsty and would go out to satiate those needs. We had organized ourselves to make sure one of us was always in the cave in case the old man came back there and wasn't able to go anywhere else to look for us. So, when I got hungry or thirsty, I just let Gavya know or waited until she got back.

Gavya would occasionally wander the oasis out of boredom and a change of scenery. Sometimes, she came back with trinkets she had found, a new type of berries to store as a snack in the cave for me, or a tale about what she had seen. The oasis was bigger than it originally appeared. Either that, Gavya said, or it was sentient and shifting for us to keep us entertained. I wouldn't wholly discount the second idea myself because, well, so much else in this place had been weird. Every once in a while, when walking around, you would get the sensation you were being watched but we never saw any other living things besides fish and other small animals. Normal animals. But whatever it felt like was watching us was not those normal animals.

Paddling around in the water by myself, I started thinking about heading back to the cave. I had left to do some hunting but got bored.

I didn't want to over-hunt this oasis and so had decided to just forage instead. My bundle of edible plants and fruits was sitting on the shore of the small lake we had found while I bathed in the water. My clothes were on a rock drying after a thorough washing.

As I slowly made my way back to the shore, I heard Gavya calling my name. "Bella, come quick!" I heard her yell out. Her tone sounded urgent, so I got my butt in gear, grabbed my clothes that weren't quite dry yet and ran to the cave. I only realized I forgot my foraging after I was inside, but oh well, I could get that later.

Inside the cave, the first thing I noticed was Gavya was not alone. The old man apparition named Nummi was back, and he was actively looking anywhere but at me. I looked down and realized I was only holding my clothes. Oops. I tossed the damp clothes to the side and Gavya handed me a part of her saree wrap to cover up. When I was decent, I walked over to the apparition.

"Have you solved the problem of how to get me and my body back together?" I asked Nummi.

"Yes," he replied, finally looking at me. "And we will do so now. Are you ready?"

I jerked a little at the suddenness of it. "Now? Right now? Really?" I asked. "Don't we need to prepare? Do I need anything? Wait!" Suddenly, a thought occurred to me. All this waiting around in the oasis for some random guy to tell me that he could put my spirit back in my body and I never considered one thing.

I turned to Gavya. "What are you going to do if I leave? You are stuck here. The Avenging Women must be after you for helping me. You can't just go back without me."

Gavya smiled slightly. "I will wait here. You go back to yourself. Make yourself whole again. Then, figure out how to come back here by your own power and blow up the plans these gods had to hold you back. We still don't know why they did it, but if you come back under all your own power, we can figure that out together. Until then, I am perfectly content to wait here."

I furrowed my brow. "Are you sure, Gavya? I don't want to abandon you when you gave up everything for me. What if I can't find a way back?"

Gavya face changed from a small smile to very serious. "I have complete faith in you, Bella. I don't know why, but I do. I also don't know what the Commission of the gods is up to, disobeying their own rules, breaking every covenant they have ever made, to treat you like they did. But I know we need to find out, and that whatever it is, it can't be good. They need to be stopped. So, if I have to wait here for a few days, or months, or hell, even years until your human form dies and you come back as a spirit that way, I will. Don't worry about me. Just come back."

I nodded and turned back to Nummi. "What do we need?"

Nummi looked around the cave. He spied a sharp rock on the ground near the firepit. Pointing at the rock, Nummi told me, "That rock, bring it here."

I followed his finger to see exactly which rock he was pointing at, grabbed it and went over to stand next to the apparition.

"Show me your arm," Nummi demanded. I knew he meant the one with the Ward in it. I held out my arm and, somehow, the amorphous figure physically touched me, tracing the scar that ran from my wrist to my elbow. "Make a cut, right there." he told me.

My mouth dropped open and I stammered. "Wait, what?"

"You stuttered, I did not." Nummi said patiently.

My brain went nuts and none of the connections between it and my mouth were working right. Do what? Cut my whole arm open. "That will hurt." I said without realizing it came out aloud.

Nummi's patience seemed to start wearing thin. "Did I give you any reason to believe it wouldn't? Did I give you any reason to think any   of   this   would   be   easy?" I shook my head no. "I think you may have even told me it would be hard, but I can't remember right now."

"I am telling you now. This will not be easy." Nummi stated firmly. "It will be hard and it will hurt. I cannot do it for you. Gavya cannot do this for you. You must do it yourself. You must open your arm and remove the Ward. Only you can do it, no one else."

My mind was both blank and reeling at the same time. A mirage of a man was asking me to physically harm myself. It dawned on me that I had no reason to trust this would work, or trust him at all.

"Why should I trust you?" I asked Nummi. "Who are you? You never really told us."

Nummi huffed and looked at Gavya. "Gavya the coordinator of the Annex, my name is Nummerion. Do you know who I am?"

Gavya gasped and put a hand to her mouth. "But you... you disappeared. You and the others disappeared from Area Two..."

"During the War, yes." Nummi interrupted her. He turned back to me. "I assume Gavya filled you in on the history of Taikarlu." I nodded, and he continued. "I don't have much time, so I will make this quick. I am one of the gods that fought on the side of the Heka in the War at Area Two. When we found out what the other gods were planning, we escaped to the human realm to regroup and plan. Now, we have been trapped there for millennia, hiding from the Joint Commission. I have learned about astral projection from my time on earth and am using it now, because the Joint Commission has been up to no good. But I am afraid the other gods will be able to figure out I am here somehow. I must hurry. Please, trust me. I am on your side."

I looked at Gavya. Her face told me that she believed him, which was enough for me. Nummi was not human, but a god who defied the Joint Commission. That made more sense than anything, but it did not ease my fear over what he was asking me to do.

Gavya must have realized why I was still hesitating. She walked over behind me. "Think of it like another Trials Arena test. They were not real. This is not real. This body," Gavya touched my shoulder, "it isn't really here. Your body is with Nummi in the human world. What you cut is just a version of you, the way Nummi here is just a version of himself."

I turned and looked at Gavya. I whispered to her. "I'm scared."

"I know." She whispered back, her hand still on my shoulder comfortingly. "I am here with you. But you have to pass this test. Come on, sit down with me. You can do this."

Gavya and I sat on the hard stone floor of the cave, facing away from Nummi. I crossed my legs and braced my right arm on my knee, with the stone in my left hand. My left hand was shaking, and Gavya placed her hand on my left knee, showing her support. "Deep breaths," she said, "calm and collected, you can do this."

With Gavya right in front of me and Nummi behind me, watching, I pushed the sharpest point on the stone into the skin at my wrist. At first, nothing happened. Then I felt the burning. Then the pain. The searing heat in my arm was a thousand times worse than any other time. As I pulled the stone, inch by inch, closer to my elbow, watching my skin open up and start bleeding, the whole right side of my body began to throb, and I couldn't help but scream. But I didn't stop. I knew I couldn't stop. If I stopped, I would never convince myself to keep going again. I screamed and pulled the stone, blood making the stone slick as I reopened the scar that had not stopped hurting in a hundred years.

Once I had traced the entire scar on my right arm, making the cut to open it back up, I dropped the stone. My left hand was shaking, and I couldn't catch my breath. My throat was raw from screaming out the pain. Tears were running down my cheeks. I turned my head to face Nummi. I had no breath left to ask him what to do next.

"The Ward should be there, just below the skin. Find it, and pull it out." He said this without any compassion in his voice, but the softness, the worry in his eyes belied his impassiveness.

I looked back at Gavya. She smiled kindly at me, her hand still on my knee. "You can do it." she whispered to me again.

Trembling, I pushed the fingers of my left hand into the cut on my right arm. I felt a stabbing pain in my right arm as I did it, and it felt like the fingers on my left hand were being electrocuted. The Ward was fighting back. I ignored these sensations, mostly. I knew I was crying and whimpering but just let myself cry and whimper and kept pushing on. My body bent to the side, as if it was recoiling from what I was doing to myself, yet I kept going.

Pushing my fingers deeper than I thought I would have to, I finally broke through the skin layer. My fingers touched something cold and hard. I ran my fingers along it and felt the object shocking my fingertips until they felt like they were burned. The pads of my fingers started to go numb from the shocks. I knew that thing was not natural and so must be the Ward. It was slippery with blood, but I grasped it between my finger and my thumb and pulled.

And pulled, and pulled. A long, thin wire the color of gold came out of my arm. "Oh, my gods," I heard Gavya say. But I just kept pulling, crying, hoarse moans of pain escaping from me, but still pulling that gold filament wire out of my arm. The fingers on my left hand holding the gold wire were completely numb now, all sensation in them electrocuted away. Finally, with a large cracking sound and the strongest burst of pain and searing heat, the wire snapped free from my arm.

Everything went black. I could not feel, hear or see anything for a long time. I floated, blissfully free of anything. I had no pain, but more than that, I had nothing. No beginning, no end. I had no name, no parents or body or spirit. There was no Gavya, no Nummi, no up or down. Nothing existed in the universe but me. The universe did not even exist. It was peaceful. I could have stayed in the nothing for ever. Then I remembered. I had seen this nothing before. When Dad used his Heka on me in his living room months ago, before I took the Trials, I had seen this nothing. Dad had said that it was just my Heka, but it felt like something more this time. The nothing was more than nothing. It was the everything before it was everything.

Dad. The thought of him snapped my mind back, and with it came everything else. Especially the pain.

AnnaBella Part One

I was lying on the floor, that much I knew. Not in the cave anymore, but in a house. My brain felt muddled up, like there were too many memories for one person in there. Slowly, I felt everything sift itself together. I was back together as one person. Here were the memories of me in Taikarlu with Dad, and here were the memories of me on earth with Mom. All together at the same time. My mind felt weird, and slightly heavy, with the memories of both lives at the same time inside me. I could remember walking in Taikarlu, eating a gyro, at the exact same moment in time as I was also in math class taking a test on probability equations. I wonder what the probability of a situation like this would be?

Then the pain came back. And the sound. I could hear other people around me speaking harshly to each other, and it took a moment to place all of the voices. My mom's I knew right off. Another one was Nummi's. After a moment, I recognized Mari's and Ben's voices, but only partly. Apparently, being two people in two different places at once, then coming back together was going to cause some memory issues for a while.

Still lying on the floor, I could feel someone moving my arm. Slowly, I opened my eyes to see what was going on. Kneeling over me, my mother was looking down at me, her face pale. She was pleading with me to wake up. When she saw my eyes had opened, she breathed a sigh of relief. "Hold still, Anna." Mom said tersely. I knew that tone of voice. Mom used that when she was scared but didn't want me to know.

I turned and looked at my right arm and saw Ben wrapping it in heavy bandages. "It won't stop bleeding! Nothing happened to it but it won't stop." He yelled, looking over me to someone else.

I followed his line of sight and saw Mari, her cell phone in hand. "She is human, Nummi, she cannot lose so much blood! Nope, that's it, Nummi. I'm calling 911." She turned the phone to start dialing while Nummi reached out a hand to stop her.

"Give it one more minute, Mari. She will wake up." Nummi told her, the only calm one in the room, but Mari shrugged off his hand.

As I watched all the movement around me, everything slowed down. Everyone's mouths moved so slowly that the sound they were making stopped. They moved so slowly that I could look at Ben as he inhaled a breath, turn my head to see Mari, then turn my head back in time to see Ben exhale.

I heard a voice say my name. "AnnaBella."

At first, I looked around to find the source of the voice, seeing everyone around me acting like they were in slow motion. Then I realized I knew that voice. It was It, the Heka. It was the same voice I heard after I messed up test five in the Trials. The voice was inside my head. Sure, like I needed more confusion in my head, I thought.

"AnnaBella." It said again.

"Hey," I replied, not really sure how to address the thing that created all the gods. "So, um, I didn't do this. I didn't mess with time again."

I felt It chuckle. "I know. I did."

Confused, I asked It. "I thought this was bad to do. Like, people, humans could die from it."

Again, I felt It laugh. "Yes, they can. When you do it. Or at least when you do it with the understanding you have now. I know how to do it right, so they will be fine."

Oh. "How, um, how can I help you? I mean, what do you need? Or what can I...?" I stumbled over my words because this was the Heka, the being, power thing that no one else had ever talked to. Well, apparently no one had talked to since the flood. Finally, I settled on just asking "What's up?" What's up? I said what's up to the maker of the universe. Gods, I cringed at myself. I felt the Heka smile slightly. "Before I tell you, you should probably heal yourself." I looked down at my arm. It was bleeding profusely. Apparently, my body hadn't gone in slow motion with everyone else's.

"I don't know how to heal myself. Can't You do it?" My head was starting to feel fuzzy, well fuzzier, and part of me was pretty sure it was blood loss this time, rather than two sets of memories in one brain.

It shook Its head and frowned, or at least I felt it do that in my head. "No, Bella. You can do it yourself. You just are forgetting you can."

I can heal myself? "How?"

"The same way you stopped time. The same way you told the test you won't needlessly kill beautiful animals anymore and made it change the program. The same way you controlled your Heka glow on the first try. The same way you forced the sand tell you where to go. Just want it, and do it." It said tolerantly, like a teacher with a struggling student.

That sounded too simple. Just want it. How could I do things like heal by just wanting it. Sure, I did the thing with time, but that was dumb luck, or bad luck since it did so much harm. The glowing was the Heka in the first place, and I didn't make the test change anything or force the sand. I just. I just did them.

"Exactly," It chimed, smiling. "You just did them. Now just heal your arm."

I looked at my arm and thought. *Stop bleeding. You are fine.* As I watched, the corners of the wound pulled together, trembled then split apart again.

It spoke again, still patient as if we had all the time in the world. As if I wasn't slowly bleeding to death. "You have to mean it."

I took a deep breath, and looked inside myself. A long time ago, or really only a few months ago depending if you are counting from Bella's time or Anna's, I would find my Heka by looking for the ice and warm in the pit of myself. I wondered if it was still there. Breathing slowly, I found it. The warm had cooled and the ice had started melting but with one small, mental poke, they both came back. Roaring back. Achingly, heart throbbingly, passionately back. Filling me up until it almost took over me. Until I almost lost sight of myself in it and actually had to ask it to slow down, back off a little. I asked the it to back off until I felt the same way that that I had with Dad that day in his living room where he had to slap me to stop my glow.

I opened my eyes again and looked at my arm. The skin had almost completely knitted itself back together, leaving a small, fine scar. I watched as the last bit healed and the bloody mess around it vanished.

"You could make the scar disappear too," It said idly.

"No," I replied firmly. "I want the scar. If I can do all this, this stuff, I want it there. As a reminder."

It nodded, thinking maybe that was a good idea.

AnnaBella Part Two

With my arm healed and the pain gone, my mind cleared a little more. The Anna and Bella parts of me seemed to make more sense together as one person rather than two. There were still overlapping memories that would take a bit to sort out, but I at least knew that they were both me and both were real.

"Good." It told me. "Now, I need you to come find me."

"What?" Confusion hit me at the desperation in the Heka's voice. "Come find you?"

It sighed, almost groaned. "Yes. You know the story from Gavya. After the flood, I supposedly disappeared?"

"Yeah, and the whole of Taikarlu split apart with the Waste everywhere and a whole bunch of animals most humans think are mythical disappeared." I tried to remember all the parts of the story Gavya had said, all of what she said had happened to the Heka, but that was still in the filtering of memories part of the brain.

It nodded in my head, a strain I hadn't noticed in the Heka before becoming more evident. "I did not disappear. I was captured."

"Captured? How?" I did not understand how the being who created everything could be captured.

If I thought it was possible, I would have thought the Heka was fighting back tears. "I gave my creations too much power. The flood was someone else's doing, not mine. Whoever they were, they were not happy with the way I did things. Instead of talking to me or asking if we could rework the system to something they thought was fairer, they captured me. They devised a plan to lock me away, where I don't know. Gods like Nummerion tried to stop them but failed. Now I am stuck. I have been able to see and know everything that has happened since and control some small things, but I am stuck here, alone. I need you to find me. I need you to rescue me."

"How? How do I go back to Taikarlu? If I leave my body to go there, the gods can just trap me again. And how do I find you if even you don't know where you are?" Too much, this was too much to ask of me. I knew nothing, and the Heka wanted me to rescue It?

"Take your body," It really was crying now, I thought. "If you can self-heal, like you just proved you can, your physical body can survive in Taikarlu. AnnaBella, I made you to do this for me. You figure out how to do the impossible every time because you are literally made for this. Like with the sand to find the oasis, like finding all the right information at just the right time in an infinite library. You can do it because you are made to." The desperation the Heka was feeling pressed down on me like a weight. Its absolute trust in me, too.

"You made me?" I questioned It. "You made me to find you?"

It looked at me closely, or well, looked at my mind. "Do you think that your father, who never wanted kids, never had any desire for millions of years even when everyone else he knew was having them, really just out of the blue decided to go down there and have one because he was lonely? No. That was me. The coordinators and gods that still thought of me in Taikarlu, still believed in me, I could come to them the same way I always had. It was hard, but I made your father think he was lonely and that he wanted a child. Do you think that he went to the human realms at just the right time to meet your mother purely by chance? Again, no. That was me. Coincidence is a real thing but it happens much less often than people think. AnnaBella, this is important. I need you to do this. You need you to do this. Everyone, everywhere, here and in Taikarlu, needs you to do this."

The Heka made my father break all the rules to have me just so that someday I would be able to save It. A small part of me broke a little at this. I had been holding a grudge against Dad for everything he did. He broke the rules and I suffered because of it and he never told me the potential for that trouble. He never gave me a choice to avoid it, but lied to me. He lied about so many things. He separated Mom and me, or I was separated from him, depending on my point of view. Either way, Mom and I suffered because of his actions. I only stopped being mad at him so I could do my job in Taikarlu better, and in the human realm, Mom and I had mourned his death, all because he lied. All because he did something he knew wasn't allowed. But if the Heka made him do those things, could Dad really be blamed for it? I guessed not. I took a ragged breath, physically blowing it out as I mentally let go of my anger with him.

Then I realized what It had said. Coincidences are real but rare. Did the Heka let my imprisonment as a spirit happen and my body suffer on purpose? I asked It that.

"No," Its anger was sharp, jagged and palpable. The Heka went from fear and anguish to white hot rage in a blink. "That was someone else. I did not want that to happen. When you were arrested and put in jail by the Avenging Women, my connection to you was lost. They built that place to block the Heka, to block me. When you came out of there, the Ward acted like a mini-prison. I could not find you to guide you until you took the Ward out. Now I see what they did to you through your memories, both the Bella ones and the Anna ones. I am angry at what they did. Furious. What they did was wrong, and they will suffer for the pain they put you through. But I can do nothing about it from here. Find me AnnaBella. Find me."

As quick as that, It was gone. Mom and Ben and everyone started moving at normal speed again. They were all speaking and arguing like no time had passed. I sat up.

"Stop," I told them. But no one heard me. So, I said it louder, "STOP!"

Everyone looked at me. Ben stopped fussing with my arm, noticing the wound was gone. Mari lowered the phone, never finishing dialing for help. Nummi smiled.

Mom's face was pale as she talked to me. "Anna, baby, are you ok? Your arm is hurt so badly, I am so worried."

I held up my arm to show her that it was fine now. She squeaked in surprise, "How?"

"I healed myself, Mom." I told her. "The Heka showed me how."

"The what?" Mom's eyes flicked from me to Nummi, confused.

"Mom." I put a hand on my mother's cheek, comfortingly, making her look at me. "You know what. The Heka. The power that made Dad. The power I inherited from him that you agreed to let him test over the summer so I could work with him in the city of the gods."

Mom looked at me askance, dubious. "Anna, your dad worked downtown for a law firm, not in any city of the gods. And he didn't have any powers that you inherited." Mom turned her gaze from me to Nummi, again. She furrowed her brow, concerned that maybe I wasn't all right even if I wasn't bleeding anymore.

"Yes, he does, Mom." I said more firmly, my hand still on her cheek. "Remember." Then it dawned on me. The Anna part of me thought Dad was human and died over the summer. I only knew that wasn't true because of the Bella part of me returning without the Ward. The gods probably made Mom forget too.

"Mom," I repeated, pushing a tiny bit of Heka into the cheek I was touching. "I need you to remember. Remember."

Mom's face went from confused, to surprised, to angry. "Anna! What happened?" Mom jumped away from me, clutching her head in her hands. "Oh, what is this?" Mom was experiencing the same heavy weirdness I had when I first put both parts of me together. She had to sort the memories out, the ones where Dad died and I almost did and the ones where she went on her trip and I spent the summer with Dad. Who knows what her memories of after the summer until now, when I was working in Taikarlu would be.

"Just relax, Mom." I told her, taking her hands into mine. "It is easier if you are calm and relaxed. Just let the memories try to sort themselves out. Don't try to force it."

Mom took a deep breath and blew it out slowly. She did this a few more times. "Feel better?" I asked her.

She nodded yes. Then, no. "What happened, Anna?" Mom asked me, angrier than I had ever seen her. "Your father was taking you to be tested. He told me it was safe, that nothing could actually hurt you in the test. If he let anything happen to you…"

I cut Mom off. "It wasn't him, Mom. I mean, it was, but not in the way you think. A lot of stuff happened, we got arrested and I have been there for a hundred years. Or, well, my spirit was."

"AnnaBella Cain, you were gone for exactly one hour!" Mom said very tersely. "You hugged me goodbye, hopped into your father's car, and then one hour later I got the call from the hospital about the accident. You were not gone a hundred years. I think I would know if you were."

I shook my head. "I am not explaining this well. The test was twelve weeks, then we were arrested, but you wouldn't have known that 'cause time is funny. So, I was here and I wasn't here, you know? I blamed Dad because he lied to you about being allowed to have a kid and that you would think I died, but now I know you thought only Dad died because part of me was here. But the Heka told me it wasn't Dad's fault. The Heka made Dad want a kid and someone else screwed up everything with me being here but not here."

Mom interrupted me again. "You are making no sense. Your father is dead. I saw his car. There is no way he survived." Mom was about to say more but then stopped. Her face looked confused as she shook her head. She continued speaking, still angry but not as harshly. "No, he wasn't human. I know that he isn't human, so why did I think he died in a car crash?"

Suddenly, I remembered everyone else around us. I looked around and saw them all pretending not to watch Mom and me discussing this. Ben was sitting on his heels to my side, slowly picking up the first aid stuff he had been using on my arm. Mari was standing by the couch that had been pushed up against one wall of the living room, pretending to be looking at something on her phone but actually looking back and forth between me and Mom, while Albert was peeking out of the kitchen door, surveying the mess in the living room. Nummi was watching me, beaming.

They all seemed to be waiting for me to do something. I suddenly realized that I had no idea what Ben, Mari and Albert knew about what was going on. Nummi had at least some clue, but I didn't even know if the others were gods or humans or what, let alone what they knew about me.

"Okay," I breathed slowly. "So, it seems there is a whole bunch of info we are all missing from one another that we totally need to talk about but, first, I think Mom needs a little break. Probably needs to be clued in to some things."

Mom snorted. "A little, yeah."

I ignored her and continued. "Nummi, I feel like you and I should talk, but Mom needs some help here too."

Nummi turned to Mari. "Will you take her?"

Mari nodded, then went over to Mom, helped her stand, and escorted her to kitchen for some tea and a private conversation, adult to adult.

I stood and moved to the couch to sit. Ben joined me there, while Nummi and Albert sat on the love seat across from us. We all sat there for some time just looking at each other.

Finally, I spoke up. "I think it would help if I knew more about all of you. You know, who you are, how many of you are actually gods instead of humans, or potentially coordinators. The basics, or whatever." I expected Nummi to talk, or maybe even Ben, so it surprised me when Albert was actually the one to begin.

"So, actually, all of us are gods. Nummi, Ben, and Mari are old-world gods. Ben said he had told you that his family, that we practiced an old religion almost nobody knew about and rarely anyone practiced anymore, right?" Albert said.

I nodded to him that yes, that was how Ben had explained it, and he continued. "In fact, Ben and Mari are gods from such a religion instead of worshippers of those gods. Nummi is from a belief system even older, one that people have not worshipped in millennia. I, on the other hand, am from a faith not yet invented. In the future, there will be a religion based around both science and faith, built from the world of science fiction stories. It will kind of be like the religion of what most people would call nerds today." Albert stopped to chuckle, then continued, asking, "How much of the history did you learn while in Taikarlu?"

I thought for a second, still putting back together my memories from my time with Gavya and my memories of high school. "Gavya told me a lot of it. Long story short, though, I know the Heka walked around with the gods for a while, then people got upset over the power distribution, then there was a fight at Area Two over who would be in charge. Some gods wanted the Heka to stay in power. Other gods thought that they should be in charge. They fought, but no one side could win. There was a flood, the Heka disappeared, and now everything is under the Commission."

Nummi, Ben, and Albert nodded. Nummi spoke next, "That is the long and short of it. I was at the battle of Area Two, fighting on the side of the Heka to take full control again. What most people don't know is that some of the gods fighting on the side of the gods taking over were actually spies for us fighting for the Heka. We got intel from these spies that there was a plan to force the Heka's hand somehow. We were told some of the gods on that side were going to leave the battle and do something; we knew not what. But their leaving was to be a signal that the plan was going to start. I was one of the ones who left the battle to follow them."

Nummi stopped talking for a moment and closed his eyes. I leaned forward, intent, hoping he would start again. But Nummi just sat there slowly shaking his head and rubbing his knees.

Finally, I got too impatient and asked, "What happened? What were the overthrowers planning?"

"It was a trick." Ben said quietly. "The spies had been found out and the Heka supporters had been deceived. The overthrowers had built a place that restrained all Heka power use within it. You know the place. It was the jail you were held in."

"Oh." I whispered quietly, picking at the fabric of the couch.

"Yeah," Ben rubbed his hands together, as if warming them against the cold of the conversation. "The Heka supporters followed the overthrowers into the jail, and they were trapped. They didn't know that the overthrowers had designed a Ward to protect themselves from the jail's power, so they all went in but only the overthrowers could leave. That was their plan, to make gods on the side of the Heka leave the battlefield. They thought that when they returned, their side would be powerful enough to overtake our side. Or if not, that they would be able to eventually trick all the gods on our side into the jail and win by default."

"Wait." I interrupted, turning sideways in my seat to look at all three of them. "The Ward I had kept my Heka away from me. Gavya said they had been used before on children of gods and humans that were crazy to stop them from doing harm. How did the gods who wanted to overthrow the Heka use them to keep their power?"

"We don't know." I focused on Albert, who had answered me this time. "They must have reverse engineered it or something. One of the things I have been working on for the last thousand or so years has been how they used the Wards in reverse. I have not gotten very far."

I turned back to Nummi. "How did you get out? When I was in there, there was nothing. No Heka, no cold and hot feeling that I had used before. Time felt like it didn't exist, even. I have no idea how long I was in that jail, earth time or Taikarlu time."

Nummi sighed, rubbing his face. His eyes looked far away, like he was lost in the memory of that time. "We don't know that either. It was such an awful time in the jail. Horrible, lonely and cold. Each of us isolated and alone. Then, all at once, it was reversed. We had all of our Heka back. The doors to the jail opened and we ran out. By that time, the flood was already over and the Wastes had been created. All of us who had been in the jail ran. We fled to the human realms and hid, eventually finding other gods who had fled at one point or another as well and we all ended up in these little groups all over the world."

"But the time in there was like nothing I have experienced before. It was nothing. It was emptiness. It was like being in the universe before there was a universe. Everything was loud, but quiet. It felt as if we were being ripped apart and pushed into the smallest atom all at the same time. Then, it just exploded around us and we were back. It had been forever and only a second, infinity in a moment." Nummi looked down and away, the memories obviously painful.

Nummi's description was so similar to mine. It was what I saw when the Heka talked to me just a few minutes ago, but without the pain he was describing. It was also where I went when Dad had tested my Heka the first time so long ago. Or, a few months ago, whatever.

"I experienced that nothing place, Nummi." All three of them looked at me sharply. "Actually, I have gone there twice. Once was just a minute ago when I healed my own arm, or really, right before I did."

Nummi, Ben and Albert all, at the same time, opened their mouths and started to say something, then seemed to think better of it. Albert actually spoke first. "The best as we have figured, that place is the place with the absence of Heka. Were you using Heka when you went there?"

I nodded. "Yeah. The first time was the time Dad had me tap into the Heka the first time, and the second time was when I removed the Ward and got my Heka back in my spirit form."

Albert stood up and started pacing. "A place with an absence of Heka only accessed when an abundance of Heka is used… Hmm." He walked back and forth slowly for a moment, while the rest of us just watched him. Finally, he stopped and shook his head. "But Nummi and the others weren't using an abundance of Heka when they got trapped in the jail. So, that's not right."

Suddenly, Ben jumped up and spoke very fast. "What if Nummi and the other Heka supporters weren't the only ones lured into the jail? What if the Heka Itself was too?"

Nummi shook his head. "No, Ben. The Heka trapped in a Heka-eliminating place would have done immense damage. A world made from It would not be able to function without It flowing freely in it."

"But the world didn't function!" Ben replied more excitedly. "It flooded. The world, on the earth, in Taikarlu, everywhere, it flooded. Cut off from the Heka, the world broke."

Albert got excited with Ben, the idea catching on. "Exactly! If the Heka's physical manifestation, and thus Its spirit that It had contained into that physical manifestation, was trapped in the jail with you, It would not have been able to continue projecting Heka into the world and the rest of the world would have broken trying to run on only the residuals left to it. Wait!" Albert's face went from excited to confused.

Albert resumed pacing for a few moments, then he slapped his forehead. "That's how they did it! The gods bent on overthrowing the Heka had reverse Wards. Their Heka would not have dissipated out of them because It was trapped in them, so while the rest of us leached Heka, using up what little stores we had, they remained fine. They could trap the Heka, let everything break just enough for their needs. Then when the time was right, they were able to release the Heka's physical manifestation because they weren't trapped suspended in either the jail or the floods like the rest of us."

Nummi nodded. "And with the world that broken, all the other gods would have been weak and wounded. The damage done to Taikarlu and the human realm would have made all the unknowing gods and coordinators scared. Albert, you and Ben and Mari were already gone by this point, so you would not have seen it, and those of us in the jail were too intent on getting away, we failed to see it. The gods who had trapped us would have been stronger and able to force everyone else to follow their plans."

What they were saying made sense, but I saw one flaw to their ideas and told them so. "You said the only way they could have stopped the flood and the damage and stuff was to release the Heka. So, how would they convince the rest of everybody to follow them if the Heka was free again? Wouldn't the Heka have just taken back control and zapped the gods who had trapped It or something?"

Ben and Albert sat down again. They and Nummi were thinking hard, I could tell. Then the answer came to me as quick as the problem had. "Unless," I began. "Unless, they didn't really release the Heka. They just made the Heka power able to come out without the Heka Itself being able to move or do anything."

Ben threw his hands up and groaned. "Well, how did they manage that?"

All three gods were looking at me, expectantly. I looked from Ben's face, to Nummi's, to Albert's. In each of them, I saw defeat and sadness, tinged by hope. It was the hope that broke me. Each of them was a god. These gods, these powerful beings, were looking at me to solve how the whole world had been broken. I stood there, thinking, for what felt like forever.

Finally, I couldn't take it anymore. "Would you stop staring at

131

me?" I said tersely. They three looked at each other, then back at me. Nummi moved as if to speak, but I didn't give him the chance. "No!" I shouted. "Why are you looking at me like I have to solve it all? I can't!" As I said this, Mom and Mari came out of the kitchen.

Mom was drying her hands on a towel as she asked, "What's the shouting for?"

"Ask them." I cried out. I started pacing, panic setting in. "They tell me stories of what happened, then look at me to solve it. Gavya steals papers and expects me to know how to solve her problems too. The Heka tells me less than nothing, then wants me to save It. I don't know how. I don't know ANYTHING!" My heart was racing by this point and, not able to do anything else, I ran out of the house into the cold night air.

I let the screen door slam behind me and stood on the front stoop. It had grown late. The quiet street was dark, with only a few houses still showing light out of their front windows. Breathing hard, I looked up at the sky. This late in winter, it was rare not to have the sky covered in clouds, but this night, the sky was blissfully clear. The light pollution from the town obscured some of the stars, but there was enough darkness for the pattern visible to be beautiful. I sat down on the stoop and stared at the sky, wishing I knew what I was supposed to do.

After a while, I realized someone was standing on the porch behind me. I lowered my head, looking at my knees, wrapping my arms around them to hug myself against the cold. "I'm sorry for shouting." I said quietly.

"Sweetheart." Mari said gently. "Don't apologize. The things you have been through just tonight would break most anyone, let alone the last six months. I'd say, all in all, you are handling it very well."

I scoffed at this thought. "The last six months? Huh, yeah. Or hundred years if you use Taikarlu's calendar."

I felt Mari walk behind me and place a warm blanket around my shoulders. I looked up, gave her a half-hearted smile by way of thanks, and pulled the blanket closer around me. The night was really cold, I suddenly realized, really, really cold.

Mari sighed the way a mother would when her child says

something disheartening. "A hundred years? Did they really have you up there that long?"

The kindness in Mari's voice sent me over the edge and I began to cry. "A hundred years." I said, letting the tears just fall. "I didn't know anything I was supposed to, the stuff all Taikarlu people know. Gavya was trying to teach me at the end there, but there was just so much stuff. And I was missing my mom. But the other side of me, my body I guess, was here missing Dad. The Trials were a mess. I did well, really well, I guess. But then the trial in front of the gods and all that happened, and I didn't know anything they expected me to. And then all this stuff about the war the gods went through, and I don't know anything. And then all this about the Heka being missing or lost or trapped somehow and It wants me to free It. And I still don't know anything. I have so many questions and no answers but everyone is looking at me like I should just know it all and fix it all with just a wave of my hand because I fixed my arm and the Heka talked to me, but I don't know anything, Mari. I just don't."

Mari didn't speak but just pulled me into a hug and held me while I cried. She stroked my hair and made shushing noises until I was all cried out. Then she still held me.

Finally, I sat up, pulling only partly out of Mari's embrace. "The thing I keep thinking is," I said when I could speak again, "that somehow, I feel like I am supposed to fix everything. Like I should know how, but as hard as I try to figure it out, I have no idea what I should do."

"Why should you know what to do?" Mari asked gently.

I thought then said "Because the Heka thinks I do."

Again gently, Mari asked, "Why do you think the Heka thinks you do?"

This question made me pause for a moment. Why did the Heka believe I knew how to save It? Why else would It ask me to do it unless It thought I could? It told me I could heal my arm and It was right about that. I mean, It was the Heka. It made everything. Maybe It knew what I didn't know I knew. This was the only answer I could come up with, and told Mari so.

"So," Mari said slowly, "if the Heka asked you to do something, and the Heka would only ask you to do it if It thought you could, and the Heka made everything, is still making everything, don't you think that the Heka would know exactly what you are and are not capable of and only ask you to do something if you really could do it? That either, somewhere inside of you, you already know the answers or the Heka will give you the answers when you need them? Don't you think you should trust the Heka?"

I pulled back more to look Mari in the face. "But I'm not smart enough. I really don't know the answers. The Heka is wrong. I have too many questions and not enough answers."

"Maybe that's exactly why the Heka knows you can do it, find It and save It." Mari replied more firmly. "Because you, AnnaBella Cain, have questions. Who else is asking the questions? Who else was asking these questions before you came along?"

I stared at Mari, dumbfounded. I had not considered that having questions, and not knowing everything already could be a good thing. The guys inside, Mari, Gavya, even my dad had all been there for all of this. They had been there first after the Heka made everything, and been there when the gods broke everything. Maybe me not being there, and me not being given all the answers in Taikarlu, meant I would ask the questions they wouldn't think to ask. They thought they knew everything there was to know about it all already. I knew nothing, and knew I knew nothing, so I would ask the questions that seemed silly or inconsequential.

Mari saw in my face that I understood now. "So, ask the questions."

I thought for a moment. What was the most pressing question I had? After everything I had heard and seen, what did I really want to know? "Why was Ben in my Trials?" was all I came up with.

Mari looked at me questioningly. "He wasn't." she answered.

"He was, twice." I told her.

Mari shook her head emphatically. "No, he wasn't. The Trials Arena is like a computer simulation. The people, or gods, in it aren't really them. They are just a generated image of them, a facsimile."

I sat up straighter and thought. For some reason, this issue of Ben felt very important to me. "But he was there. I talked to him twice.

Once, we fought the multi-headed snake and he got poison dripped on him. It made the same scars he has now. Scars, I'm assuming, he hasn't actually been missing school to go to doctor's appointments for?" I stopped and thought on that for a moment. Would Ben have even needed to go to school if he is actually an ancient god? Probably not. So, why was he? Questions for later, I thought. "In the second test, he had a dog named Fury that was attacked by birds and almost died. There was also a lady with a pet deer who my dad said was mean but was really nice to me, a con artist guy who tricked me, a lady with apples that I never actually talked to, some teenagers, a horde of angry soldiers and my dad. And none of that includes the animals I talked to."

Mari's eyes were wide when I finished speaking. Her voice came out hoarse when she croaked out, "You spoke to animals in your Trials? Did they... did they speak back?"

I sat for a moment, trying to remember. "No. Not exactly. I didn't speak to the lion, but I spoke to the test after I killed the lion and told it I wouldn't skin it anymore, and the test listened to me. But that was before I knew it was all a simulation."

I stopped and thought a bit more. I didn't speak to the snake, the deer, or the boar. "I talked to Fury when we were fighting the birds and Cerberus while I put him to sleep, but I talked to them the way people talk to dogs, nothing special. But the bull and I talked. Well, kind of. He showed me images in my mind and I kind of thought-spoke to him too. Oh yeah, I spoke to villagers twice, the king and his guard and the ferryman but those were all people."

Mari was staring off, thoughtfully. "You spoke to some of the animals, that's normal. But you spoke with the bull. You spoke and he responded, like a real conversation in its own way."

"Yep." I replied. "Why? Is that weird? I mean, it can't be the weirdest thing I did in the Trials. I mean, I did speak with the Heka during the Trials and that kinda freaked a lot of people out."

Mari spoke slowly, as if she was cautious of saying the wrong thing. "Speaking with the bull isn't necessarily weird, per se, but how you describe it is. Speaking with the villagers, the king and the ferryman are normal too, like talking to Cerberus and the person fighting the bi-headed snake and the woman with the deer. I have never heard of Fury being used in the tests before, but then not many people talk about how they completed each individual test." Mari stopped and I waited to see if she would say more.

She did, suddenly sitting bolt upright as if she had been startled. "How did you get Fury in the test with the birds if you just spawn into a random village for that one? How did you find Ben to get to Fury?"

I shrugged. "I looked for him. I recognized the houses from the test with the snake and asked around. Ben had Fury with him when I found him, and it gave me the idea to use the dog to hunt the birds."

Mari suddenly reached over and kissed the top of my head. "AnnaBella Cain, you are a genius!" She stood and ran quickly in the house.

Confused, I got up and followed her. Inside, my mom was sitting with the three gods discussing the real meaning of the ancient cave drawings (apparently, most of them are just an old version of movie night). All four of them looked up at Mari as she went to stand between them, declaring loudly, "AnnaBella asks questions."

Albert was the first to respond to this seemingly out of place statement. "Okay. And?"

Mari shook her head, indicating they didn't understand. "No, AnnaBella asks questions all the time. She asks animals questions, like the bull in the Trials. She asks coordinators questions, like Gavya while she was in Taikarlu for a hundred years. She asks gods questions, like Nummi, and Ben." She stopped and took a breath before beginning again, with more emphasis. "Like she asked the villagers in one of the Trials tests so that she could purposely find Ben."

The three other gods had been listening curiously until Mari mentioned Ben being in the Trials with me. Then everyone looked at Ben shocked, and Ben jumped up excitedly.

"You looked for me in the Trials?" he stammered. "Why?"

All eyes turned to me. The four gods looked at me with surprise and excitement. My mother looked at me with confusion, which I could understand because I was confused too. I kept my eyes on Ben as I followed Mari to the center of the living room. "Because you had been nice to me in a previous test, the one with the snake, and I recognized that the test with the birds was the same village as that test and thought maybe you could help me again. You did, if that matters."

Mari again shook her head. "No. Tell him who really helped you."

"Fury." I stated. "Fury helped me. You helped by letting me borrow Fury."

"Um, can someone explain this to me." Mom piped in. "I have no idea what is going on."

"Me either." I muttered under my breath.

Ben answered my mom. "The Trials are made up of twelve tests. Twelve individual tests that have nothing to do with one another. But Anna looked for me in a different test that the one my visage is usually used in and found me."

"Wait." I cut in. "They are not all individual. I also called in the pelt from the lion from the first test so I could use it for the test with the birds with my door."

"Your door?" Nummi asked me.

"Um, yeah. Sorry." I explained. "My Heka. Dad said you got one time to get supplies for each test, and when I called on the Heka for my supplies, it came from a door appearing. I would open the door, take the stuff out of what looked like an empty closet, then close the door. Then the door would just disappear."

There were several soft "Ohhh" noises as everyone looked at each other, and I heard Nummi say "Mine came in a bucket" and Albert say "I typed my needs on a computer and 3D printed them."

Ben and Mari both started pacing the open space of the living room, passing each other without interrupting the other's stride. Ben spoke as he paced. "You used things, and me, from one test in another. Mari said you asked the bull questions. I assume that means the bull answered?"

I nodded to say he was right, and Ben kept talking. "None of that should have been possible. The Trials was made for each test to be completely separate. But that is not the only thing you did in the Trials that was impossible. You inverted time. You spoke to the Heka."

Now it was Mari's turn to interject. "The goddess of the hunt was apparently nice to her."

Ben stopped midstride. "The goddess of the hunt was nice to you. That may honestly be the strangest thing you did in the Trials, believe it or not. The goddess of the hunt doesn't like anybody, especially when her deer is missing. Simulation or not, she is very ornery."

"So, I did weird things during the Trials. We knew that. We all knew that. Heck, I talked to the Trials itself and it listened. So what? What does it matter? What does it mean?"

Everyone was surprised when Mom answered me. "It means that you could control the Trials with your power, this Heka. From what little I know, from what Mari and your dad explained, no one can control the Trials. Not even the three gods who made the Trials can control them after they set it going."

"And if you can control the Trials," Nummi finished for Mom, "then what else can you control?"

Albert picked up from there. "Maybe you could control the gods, make them answer your questions."

"If I could control the gods and make them answer my questions," I sat down on the arm of one of the couches, frustrated, "wouldn't I be doing that now? And wouldn't I have been able to do that before they put the Ward in me? And if I can, but didn't because I didn't know I could, what does that make me?"

Ben and Mari sat down right where they stood, in the middle of the living room floor, and everyone else slumped in their seats as if the thinking all of this out had made them weary, because they didn't have the answers to those questions. My mind was going a million miles an hour with questions I couldn't even fully form. I looked at each of them. My mom, Ben, Mari, Albert, and Nummi. They all were slightly slumped, their eyes slightly downcast, each one rubbing their face or their arms. Gradually, each one turned their face towards me. They all looked at me expectantly.

I could control things that no one, not the gods, not the coordinators, no one could control. A thought began to brew in the back of my mind. The only thing that used to be able to control the gods was the... Nope. I didn't like where it was going, so I shoved that thought down with a force of will. Not going there, not a chance. Instead, I focused on something else.

I focused on asking more questions. "If" I queried, "and that is a big if, I can control everything, why did I choose Ben twice in the Trials? Why did I make the bull talk with me? And why did I make the goddess of the hunt nice to me?"

"So, you would know them and be comfortable with them." Again, Mom with the simple, logical answer. "Because you knew then that you would need them later. You needed Ben to know Nummi to get set free from the Ward. Maybe you need him for something else too. I don't know what you need or needed the goddess of the hunt or the bull for, though."

Albert then spoke softly, almost too softly. "The goddess of the hunt is our man on the inside."

"What?" I asked, not hearing him well.

Albert cleared his throat, and repeated himself. "The goddess of the hunt is our man on the inside. She fought with the gods against the Heka during the war, but was actually on the Heka's side. She was a spy. Since we left Taikarlu, she has been feeding me and a few others information. Like she told me that your father had a child and you both were arrested. And that you were charged to come back to earth as a human, and we should look for you because there was something not right about that. Because she swore she saw you in Taikarlu after you were supposedly sent back. She is a spy for those of us on the side of the Heka and has been all along. I don't know how you could have possibly known that, but somehow you did. Maybe the Heka was helping you, subconsciously nudging you to the right people."

"Is that why you were in high school with me?" I asked Ben. "Even though you are an ancient god and don't need to learn algebra?"

Ben nodded. "The fact that I have the scars helped because, with your medical stuff, it made you trust me more since I had medical stuff too. I could keep an eye on you, help you if you needed, especially once we figured out the whole separated body and spirit thing. The doctors' appointments ruse just gave a good cover for when I went to do god stuff."

That made sense. "And the bull?" I asked, expecting them to say there was something special about that animal too.

All four of the gods shrugged. I looked to Mom, who had figured so much out herself, and she only shrugged as well. I let out a terse sigh. "We can figure out the bull later, I guess." Or maybe the bull was just a bull.

"What now?" Albert asked.

Nummi held up a hand to stop me from saying anything. "Before you answer, AnnaBella, think. You know the questions to ask, apparently, and may have a lot more control of things in either Taikarlu, earth or both than you think. You know what to do, even if you think you don't. Ask yourself the question. What should we do now?"

My answer of I have no clue died on my lips. I did know. I had to go back to Taikarlu. I had to confront the gods about what they did to the Heka during the flood. And I had to do it fast. Nummi had made it clear that the gods sometimes, somehow knew what was up in the human realm. If they knew what I was up to, they may figure out how to stop me from coming back.

My mind was filling with doubts. How could I possibly get back now that my spirit and my body were back together? If I could control everything, I guess I could just go back to the building downtown Dad took me to when I visited Taikarlu during the summer and just make the door work for me. How would my body survive in Taikarlu? Again, control. I could just control it, right? I didn't have time to think it all out. I had to act and hope I wasn't wrong.

"Mom, I need you to drive us somewhere." I suddenly said.

"Us?" Mom questioned.

"Ben and me. We need to go now." I responded, walking to the coat closet and grabbing my coat. I grabbed Ben's and threw it at him. "If I decided in the Trials that you were necessary, Ben, you must be necessary. So, hurry up."

Ben fumbled around to catch his coat and shrugged it on as he moved to catch up with me. "Where are we going?"

"The building on A Block Row. Then Taikarlu. We need to get answers out of the gods and we need to do it before they have any clue what I am up to. You in?" I stated, very matter-of-fact.

Ben grinned wickedly. "Oh, I am so in." He went down the front stairs two at a time, pulled open the front door of the house, and turned back. "Hey, um, AnnaBella's mom? We don't need you after all. Guess AnnaBella really can control things how she wants."

I looked down the stairs, around Ben, through the door and saw the foyer of the Central Hub where the front porch should have been. The stories-tall statue of a man and woman was there, moving through fighting, embracing and dancing as it always had, but the rest of the foyer was empty. There were no gods or coordinators or visitors milling around like there usually was. The hair on the back of my neck stood up and I realized we were too late.

The gods must know already. They were probably all in the room with the silver door, waiting for me. Well, nothing to it but to do it, I thought, and I prepared myself to walk though yet another door.

Book Two: Healed

The Quartet

Taikarlu and the Central Hub was right there through Ben's front door. I knew the moment I stepped through the Avenging Women would sense my return and come after me. But there was nothing for it but to do it. I took a deep breath and lifted my foot, ready to step through.

Nummi put a hand on my shoulder and stopped me. "Not you first." I gave Nummi a questioning look and he continued. "You want to go in with your human body?" I nodded yes. "Let us go first. You are going to have to stretch your Heka to cover all of us, protect all our bodies from disintegrating in Taikarlu. If you fail, we won't be harmed since our bodies are just creations for us to walk around in the human world that we discard to go back to Taikarlu anyway. You? Your human body would not survive and that could make the issues much worse."

"What do you mean us?" I looked at him quizzically.

"Us." he repeated firmly. "Ben and myself. Albert and Mari, too, if they want. Did you think I would let you go alone? Just you and Ben? I fought for the Heka thousands of years ago. I will continue fighting today. My body may look old, but there is god enough left in me to go another few rounds."

Nummi looked at Albert, who squared his shoulders and pushed his glasses back up onto the bridge of his nose. His determined face told me he would come along.

Mari, on the other hand, looked at Mom and seemed torn. "Nummi, I want to go," she began.

Nummi, sensing what Mari was going to say, interrupted her. "On second thought, Mari, maybe you should stay here with AnnaBella's mother. With the time differences and everything else, she will need the support of someone who understands."

Mari breathed a small sigh of relief at the same time as Mom did. Looking from one woman to another, I could tell they had bonded during their time in the kitchen. It would be good for Mom not to be alone with all this.

Everything decided, Nummi shouldered past me and confidently walked through the doorway. At first, I thought I would have to make some effort, hold some kind of intense concentration, to keep the power in Taikarlu from affecting his human body. Instead, I started emitting a faint glow without even being conscious of doing it. The glow emanated from me outward towards Nummi and settled on him, like a long cloak draping around his shoulders, turning into a faint shimmer that faded in the Taikarlu light.

After a moment of watching Nummi across the threshold, Albert pushed past me and I watched him walk through the door. The shimmer spread from Nummi and settled over him. Then it was Ben's turn. He walked through the door and the shimmer again expanded to cover him. The shimmer on both gods almost vanished in the light of Taikarlu.

Finally, it was my turn. I took a deep breath and lifted my foot yet again to cross the threshold of the door. And yet again, a hand fell on my shoulder to stop me. This time, though, it was my mom's.

"Wait." Mom's voice was soft, just barely shaking. "Before you go, I want to say something."

I turned to face her. For a moment, I worried that turning away would break the spell over the three gods who had gone through the doorway but a quick glance over my shoulder proved to me they still held that faint shimmer.

Mom took a steadying breath. "Anna, I just want to say I love you. My memories are still a little confused, and a lot of this stuff does not make complete sense to me, but I know everything from that world and this are not quite in sync. I also know you are going to do some pretty intense stuff with some people… no, not people, some gods who really aren't going to be happy about it. These people, these gods," she gestured to Nummi, Mari, Albert and Ben, "seem to believe you can fight them, and would be right to fight them. More than that, they seem to believe you can win and make the world better by doing so."

Mom shook her head slightly, as if clearing away some thought. "I don't know them. I don't even know if I really trust them. But I do know you. I do trust you. If you think you should do this, then I believe you that it is the right thing to do. That's all I wanted to say." Mom paused, then added, "Oh yeah, and I love you so very, very much." Mom pulled me into a tight hug, her face resting on my hair. She sniffed once and then let me go.

"Go." Mom whispered and pushed me gently toward the door.

I looked at Mom. She had to do this twice now. "I love you, too, Mom." I hugged her once more, then shut my eyes, and actually walked through the doorway into Taikarlu.

I stood on the other side of the door for a moment with my eyes still shut. I could feel the power in Taikarlu. It felt like sandpaper on my skin. At first, it itched, then felt like a friction burn. Then the feeling settled down into a slight warmth that made the hairs on my arms raise. Goosepimples skittered across my skin. Then with a deep calming breath, I finally felt normal. Well, immense power around me, but normal.

I opened my eyes and saw that the shimmer was on me too. I looked back at the door I had just walked through, and saw Mari quietly shutting it. I turned and looked into the heart of Central Hub. Nummi, Albert, and Ben stood between me and the fountain, watching me expectantly.

Other than the four of us, the place was vacant. The normal hum of conversations was absent. I had never experienced a lack of anyone in Central Hub before and it gave the place an eerie feeling. Like being at school late at night. Curious, I turned to look through the front door of the Central Hub which, now shut, reflected the main city street of Taikarlu rather than Ben's living room. With Taikarlu being a place where the sun never set, and the inhabitants were godly beings or the dead that never needed sleep, I had never experienced the emptiness that was now all-encompassing. The street outside the Central Hub was a ghost town. Instead of beings of all shapes, sizes and colors, there was no one. All that showed through the glass door was a vacant street of glass lined with buildings of gold reflecting prisms of color through the air.

I turned back to the gods who were with me. Albert spoke first.

"I would hazard that everyone is in Commission Room, which is probably not a good sign for us," he offered hesitantly.

"I would pull back on protecting us three, AnnaBella." Nummi suggested. "We do not need to retain our human forms, as I said before, but you will probably need all the strength you can muster if the gods, and everyone else in Taikarlu, are already rallying."

I agreed with Nummi. I was not intentionally protecting us, so it took me a moment of actual contemplation to figure out how to stop doing it for only some of our party. I closed my eyes and tried to find the Heka feeling inside me. It was there in my core, larger than ever, that cold and warm feeling, overpowering, raw and absolute. I realized that I desperately wanted to keep all of us safe, and that because I didn't know what was coming, my Heka had just translated that desire into a barrier around us. It took an act of will to convince my own mind that Ben, Albert and Nummi were safe without my help so that my Heka would let them go.

Finally, I was able to do it, reign in my Heka, and I opened my eyes to see the three gods no longer shimmering. I looked down at my own body and saw I still was. The faintest whisps of shimmer floating just above my skin. No one who wasn't looking for it would even know it was there. I waited a moment, watching the three of them, ready to revert my thoughts at the hint of trouble, but they all stood still showing no signs of change or pain. Their human bodies had never been real in the first place, just creations they used to make it easier to move around the human realm. I realized that meant that when their physical bodies dissolved, nothing noticeable changed about them.

Finally convinced they were okay, I decided we should move on. "Well, if everyone is in the Commission Room, then that is where we should go," I told them. Ben nodded in agreement.

The four of us started walking towards the bank of elevators on the other side of the statue. Before we got very far, I felt a familiar sensation. All of my muscles started tensing and it felt like I was walking through syrup. The Avenging Women were here.

Six of the milk white warrior women walked calmly from their hiding place behind the statue. I could tell they had been waiting to see what we did before they attempted to impose their control on us. Now, seeing that we were going to go to the Commission Room, they chose to act.

But something was different than the other times I had come into contact with them. When I was arrested at the Trials Arena, I had not been able to move at all, not even blink. When they came to me at the Annex, I could still move but how much was dependent on how close they were. Now, even though they were almost right next to me, I could still move some. My arms and legs were heavy, but I could shift my weight from one foot to another. I could turn my head to look at one Avenging Woman then another. I turned my eyes, slowly, to look at my companions. Ben was frozen in place, his chest not even moving in the imitation of breathing he did automatically. Albert looked pained, having been caught midstride with one foot in the air. He had only enough control to shift to a less uncomfortable position. If I hadn't known better, I would have thought Nummi was just casually waiting. He seemed serene and comfortable, but was not moving around either.

"AnnaBella Cain, you are under arrest for violation of your warding," one of the Avenging Woman stated blandly. The Woman who had spoken was standing in front of the others and seemed to be the leader. The other five Women were ranged in a semi-circle behind her, tensing as if they were ready to act at a moment's notice. The Women did not have any weapons out. They didn't need them because of their power to freeze anyone, including gods, in their tracks and speak to their prisoners through their minds was usually better than any weapon.

Knowing they could hear my thoughts, I had intended to counter their claim in my head, but somehow managed to move my lips enough to speak out loud. "Was my warding legal?" I asked. My power lay in my questions, they had told me, so I would question everything.

The Avenging Woman in charge made a face of perturbance. "The warding order was given after your trial by the gods. A form 22-D was properly filled out and signed by the god in charge of your punishment and witnessed by Malachi." Huh, I thought Malachi only dealt with humans and their true beliefs. I guess he had other jobs he did around here. Thoughts for another time.

"Yeah, sure. They did the right forms." I responded, allowing my irritation to seep into my voice. "But was it legal?"

The Avenging Woman in charge looked confused, and the Women behind her seemed to shift from one foot to another uncomfortably. "What do you mean legal? The god in charge of your punishment filed a form 22-D, witnessed…"

"Witnessed by Malachi, yeah, yeah." I interrupted, pushing the point. "They did all the right steps, I get that. But were they allowed to take those steps? Was that what the humans decided my punishment would be?"

Confusion was obviously not something Avenging Women were used to feeling. The Woman in charge seemed to be experiencing some form of physical pain the more confused she became. Her voice raised an octave, and seemed strained as she asked me "What do you mean humans deciding your punishment? The god in charge of your punishment filed a form 22-D, witnessed by Malachi."

They have no idea, I thought to myself. "Were you at my trial?" I asked. "Were you, yourself, there? Or do you guys have a hive mind thing like the TIMS do? Do you know, for one hundred percent certain, what my charges and punishments were supposed to be?"

The Woman in charge began to speak, repeating again "The god in charge of your punishment…" but was interrupted by one of the Avenging Women behind her.

"We do not have a hive mind like the TIMS. We are independent but bound by the laws and codes of the Commission. None of us present today were present at your trial, but are bound to act as commanded by the Commission, as directed by authorized documents witnessed by the Secretary of Religious Agency, Malachi the Good." Oh, so that was Malachi's full job. Interesting.

"So, let me see if I understand this." I said slowly. Not just because of the Avenging Women's power, but because I wanted to make the Women think, and thinking for themselves seemed to be a new, and maybe terrifying, concept for them. "A god wants to do something to someone else. All he has to do is find some applicable law that they may or may not have broken, fill out the proper form saying they did, have Malachi sign it as witness, and you guys just, what? Arrest that person with no evidence?"

The Woman at the front of the group responded. "Malachi the Good is evidence. He will only witness what is true and right. He knows a person. He knows their beliefs and desires. He knows their goings and comings. He is the Good."

An idea started to form in my mind. "What if he was wrong?" I asked. "What if Malachi the Good lied?"

In unison, the six Avenging Women spoke as if robots, standing straight and staring straight ahead at nothing. "Malachi the Good is never wrong. Malachi the Good cannot be questioned. Malachi the Good is the Good."

Woah. So, that is something to be explored, I thought. Something not good that needed to be explored later. But first, I need these Avenging Women not to arrest me and put me in the jail that blocks all Heka access.

"Ok, let me make sure I have this straight." I spoke very carefully. "None of you were at my trial, so you only know what my punishment was because of a form 22-D that was filled out by a god and signed as true and right by Malachi. This form said I was supposed to be Warded and not leave Taikarlu. I removed the Ward and left Taikarlu, so now I need to be arrested and put in jail because I broke the rules. Is that all right according to you?"

The Woman in charge nodded. "Yes. That is the truth."

"But I was not just Warded to be kept in Taikarlu. Did you know that? My human body was alive and still functioning in the human realm, on Earth or whatever. Was that part of my punishment, the separation of my human body and my spirit until my body died and my spirit was broken on form 22-D?" I asked them, looking from one Woman to another.

"You have no human form." The Woman in charge said dismissively.

"Look again." I told her, forcing my muscles to move so I can stand closer to her. "I am human now, in Taikarlu. How is my spirit in my human body if I have no human body?"

"That is not possible." she replied, her eyes turning away from me, as if to hide from what she wouldn't be able to deny if she just looked at me. "Human bodies cannot survive in Taikarlu."

"Mine is." I retorted. I stepped another step closer to her, reached out my arm, slowly, still under their compulsion to hold still, but fighting it. "Look at me, feel me. How am I moving? How am I talking when I am under your power if not because I have a human body?"

The Avenging Women's confusion increased to such a point they seemed to be squirming from the discomfort. The Woman in charge's mouth flapped open and closed like a fish. She seemed to want to say something but could not string together the words.

"Let me help you here." I shifted, making myself move so that they had no choice but to be fully aware of the fact that I could. That I was moving when I shouldn't have been able to. "In my trial, Malachi the Good declared that my faith is in humanity. Not in any specific god or religion, but humans and their implicit goodness. They said that I was at fault for going into the Trials Arena as a human that should have known better, but that they could not decide if I used the Heka wrong because that is only something the Heka Itself could decide. I was found innocent of everything else. Everything. The Speaker said that if my faith is in humans, then humans got to decide what happened to me. I had to write my story, give it to the humans and let them decide if I stayed as a coordinator in Taikarlu and my human body went away, or if I became only a human and lose all of my Heka power forever."

I let that sink in before pushing my next point. "This means the humans were in charge of my punishment. Not any god, not the Speaker, not even Malachi the Good. The humans and only the humans. And they were not given splitting me in two, and have me get both as one of their potential choices."

I stopped and took a breath. The Avenging Women seemed to be listening intently, so I continued. "What did the humans decide? Tell me, because what happened to me, and the order you were given, does not follow either choice."

For a long moment after I said this, nothing happened. The Avenging Women seemed to not move, not even blink. Then the Woman in charge turned to the other five Women. Some of them shrugged at her. One looked angry and another seemed to shrink in confusion. The Woman in charge turned back towards us and immediately I felt the pressure on me relax. The feeling that my muscles were heavy went away and my mind cleared so I no longer felt like I was moving through syrup. I heard Albert audibly sigh in relief.

"This does not make sense," the Woman in charge stated, rubbing her forehead in a way that was almost comical in its humanness.

I gave her a look of sympathy. "Welcome to my life. Nothing makes sense. But do you agree that I shouldn't be under arrest right now?"

"No," she said emphatically. "There is an order for your arrest, so you need to be arrested." She then bunched her eyebrows and twisted her mouth. "But also, yes. Your order seems to be done in error." The Avenging Woman's shoulders shrugged then sank and she seemed to lose her powerful demeanor. "I do not know anymore. I have never not known. I cannot let you go, but I cannot arrest you if it might be a false arrest either."

A part of me thought about what everyone had said back in Ben's living room. If they were right, I could just control the Avenging Women. I could just make them let me and my friends go, just make her know that letting us go was the right thing to do. If they were right that I could control everything, then I could just control the Avenging Women...

No. Absolutely not, I decided. Controlling people, or whatever the Avenging Women are, like that was not okay. Controlling anyone to do things they didn't want to was not okay. Forcing people to give me information I wanted was one thing, as long as it was only to force them to tell the truth, the real truth. Even that felt sketchy in my mind, but I knew it might be necessary at some point. But forcing someone, any sentient being, to physically do something against their will was about as wrong as wrong could get. I made the vow right then and there that I would never do that. Never. There was always another way.

"What if," Albert offered, finding that other way, "you do both?"

"How?" The Avenging Woman asked. It was almost a plea.

"Simple," he shrugged. "Don't let her go. Instead, take her to the Annex and find the records of her arrest, trial, the decision made and the new warrant for arrest. If the records show what AnnaBella says, you can be assured the warrant was invalid and let her go. If it doesn't, then you can put her in jail. She stays under your power the whole time, so she is arrested but just not taken to the jail."

The Avenging Woman shook her head. "That will not work. The Keeper of the Annex has vanished. We cannot access the records."

Shoot. I forgot about Gavya. "I can help with that. Gavya is in hiding because she helped me escape. She is in an oasis in the Wastes. The first one to the north of the Hills. We should probably let her know she is safe to come back, and that it appears we need her help."

"We cannot enter the Wastes." The Avenging Woman told us.

Nummi, of course, had the solution. "I can, and quickly." Nummi sat down on the floor and closed his eyes. After a moment or two, he opened them. "This human form of astral projection is helpful sometimes. Gavya is on her way as fast as she can. She will meet us at the Annex."

"Then let's go." I told them and the whole group of three gods, six Avenging Women and I walked out of the Central Hub and onto the empty streets of Taikarlu. So many times, I had walked this same path, usually stopping for a gyro or other food along the way and watching the people go by. But now all those shops were closed and the people were gone, probably waiting for us in the Commission Room. We didn't talk while we walked. The sounds of twenty feet shuffling along the glass pavement was all that could be heard.

We arrived at the Annex and found it was still locked shut. Unsure what to do, we all waited quietly, shuffling our feet and each of us keeping to our own thoughts. My mind kept wandering to Malachi the Good. How was he wrapped up in all this? Was he really good? Or was there more to the story? And how, after I figure out all this, was I supposed to get the gods who had locked up the Heka to tell me how to free It? I didn't want to have to force them and they obviously weren't going to just tell me because I asked nicely, or something.

Just the Six of Us

Gavya finally arrived at the Annex. I expected her to look disheveled or at least out of breath. Instead, she looked calm and her saree was clean and tidy. She had brought the backpack stuffed with papers with her. Gavya unlocked the Annex and asked what we were looking for, only giving the Avenging Women a slight glance to show they made her nervous.

Ben, Albert, Nummi and I entered the Annex and Gavya held the door open for the Avenging Women. The Woman in charge shook her head. "We will remain out here to secure the building." She stands resolutely with the five other Women behind her.

I disagreed. "You can leave the others outside, but at least one of you should come in too. How will you know we are giving you the right records, and all of the records, if you don't see it for yourself?"

The Avenging Woman in charge relied simply, "We will have to believe you."

This time Ben disagreed. "Do you, or do you not have free will?" He didn't wait for her to answer. "You do. I know because you are right now exercising that free will to defy what might be an illegal order. Keep using it and use your own rational thinking too. Come in with us, see for yourself, and use your free will and rational minds to make your own choice of what should happen next. You are not a puppet, are you?"

I could see the moment the Avenging Woman in charge changed

her mind. Her shoulders rounded as Ben's words had their impact on her. As she realized that she was, in fact, using a form of free will she had not ever considered using before. The head Avenging Woman did not make any fancy proclamations about this realization as it rolled through her but only nodded that she agreed and gave the command for the other five to surround the building. No one was to leave or enter until she said so. She and Gavya entered the building, and Gavya went straight to the restricted section.

When she returned, the bookbag was empty. She must have returned all the documents we stole to their rightful places. "Better," she said, breathing a sigh of relief and rolling her shoulders to release the tension that had built up in her. I hid a small smile at the annex-keeper and her absolute need to have everything in its rightful place in her library. She settled into her normal librarian role as if our run to freedom and hiding in exile had never happened, and continued. "Now, what are we looking for?"

"Everything pertaining to me," I told her. "From the moment my arrest warrant was issued at the Trials Arena to now, everything you can find that talks about me."

Gavya sighed. "Those record are sealed. I cannot access them."

The Avenging Woman looked at Ben. "You are the god of the highest standing here. Can you file a Form 18-X-3?"

"Wait," I said confused. "Ben has the highest standing here?"

Nummi responded. "I have no worshippers anymore. Albert does not have any yet. You and Gavya are not gods. Ben has a small tribe that pays allegiance to him still, making him the highest-ranking god here. The Avenging Women can only act if their orders are filed by a god with witness from Malachi or if enacted in an emergency by the highest-ranking god present. I do not think we want to wait and find Malachi for this."

No, definitely not. I turned to Ben and waited to see what he would do.

"I hate this," Ben muttered under his breath. He sighed and told the Avenging Woman "Can you please give me a Form 18-X-3? I declare emergent status." It was very interesting to me how, even though I now knew Ben was a god, and thousands of years old, he still sounded and acted seventeen. Even while doing something so very god-like as paperwork. It was getting really hard not to laugh.

The Avenging Woman reached inside her robes and pulled out a scroll. She handed it to Ben, who unrolling it, leaned across the desk to grab a pen. Gavya handed him one and he began filling out the long paperwork, muttering and sometimes even cursing under his breath.

While we waited, I talked quietly to Gavya. "Hey, sorry I left you so long."

"Was it long?" Gavya asked me, honestly. Her face was openly curious.

I thought for a minute. "Actually, I don't know how long it was here. I am really even kind of confused about how long it was in the human realms." Had it really only been just that morning I had told Ben that I would let his grandpa do the ritual on me? That would mean it hadn't even been a full day. But it felt so much longer. Years longer.

Gavya smiled at me. She pointed to herself. "Not human. I don't get hungry or tired or lonely. Bored, I do get bored. But that's okay. You sent for me when you needed me, exactly as you said you would. You kept me from being arrested just as you said you would. You have nothing to be sorry about, Bella."

Well, at least that was good then. Gavya wasn't mad at me, and it seemed would not suffer for helping me. One less stressor on my plate. Now I just had to worry about not being arrested myself and saving the whole world. Worlds? Whichever. No biggie.

Ben finished the paperwork and handed it to the Avenging Woman. The Avenging Woman looked it over, nodded, and handed it over to Gavya. "The paperwork has been unsealed under Form 18-X-3, with emergent order. Please produce it immediately."

Gavya went to the back of the Annex, vanished into the Restricted Section, then reappeared a moment later with a box in her arms. The box was a black rectangle, about the size of a toaster, and had a gold seal on the top. Gavya set the box down on her desk and pushed it in front of Ben.

Ben pushed his palm onto the gold seal on the top of the box and it made an audible cracking noise. When he lifted his hand, the seal was broken in two. The box split into halves, with each side falling away, leaving a pile of scrolls and sheaves of paper lying on the desk.

I grabbed a handful of the papers and started skimming over them. They were the report from the Trials Arena, with every tiny action I had taken detailed. The record included every word I or Dad said, and what other people in the tests said. It also had a scoring section after each individual test. I shuffled through, stopping to read a little here and there, until I reached a part where I saw the words "Fury."

"Hey," I said, pointing to the paper. "I told you that you were in my trials, Ben. Here, it talks about me saving your dog, Fury."

Ben took the papers from me and read some, flipping pages here and there. "Dude, Fury! He was there, not that I didn't believe you, Bella. Dang, I miss that pupper."

"What happened to him?" I asked.

Ben sighed. "The people stopped talking about him. Gods only get companions when the people believe they get companions. Unless that companion is given some sort of godlike status of their own, which means they exist forever, kind of like Cerberus. If not though, they come and go at the will of the belief of the people. Fury was a companion people believed I had for a while, so I had him. We had some great times together and the people in my tribe told the stories of our adventures often. But then, at some point, they just stopped telling the stories with Fury in them so much. Over time, people forgot about Fury and he disappeared as my companion."

"If someone told the stories again, would he come back?" Curiosity had made me distracted from the mission we were there for. But good dogs are important, so it was okay.

"Yes," Ben explained. "If only someone could remind them. I would love to have Fury back. I'm glad he was with me in the Trials, if he can't be anywhere else."

I smiled and turned back to the paperwork, deciding to talk to the Heka about how we could fix it so companions like Fury weren't lost to time anymore. I picked up another sheet of paper and saw it was the transcripts from my trial in front of the gods. Flipping through it, I found the section where the Speaker put the decision for my punishment on the humans and set it down on the desk. We would probably need to reference that later.

I shuffled through the scrolls and papers a bit more, attempting to find the record of the humans' response but not seeing it anywhere. I looked at everyone else. They all had a scroll in their hands, reading intently.

"Who has the humans' response to my trial?" I asked.

Everyone looked up, but no one said anything. "No one?" I pushed. "It is not in this pile, so one of us must have it. Where is it?"

Everyone started moving the books and papers around on Gavya's desk. There was a chorus of "Not here" and "These are just arrest papers." Finally, Gavya put her hands up and told everyone to stop.

"If we keep moving everything around willy nilly," she declared, "then we will lose more papers instead of finding what we want. Give me everything."

Everyone collected the papers in front of them and handed them to Gavya. Once she had a large stack, she started looking over each one and placing them in chronological order. Meanwhile, I picked up the extra stuff on her desk, books that she and I had left there when we ran from the Avenging Women the first time, and moved them away so we wouldn't get confused. Ben picked up the two halves of the box with the now broken seal from the floor where they had fallen and set them on the cleaned-off desk. He set them down in a way that let us see they were empty inside.

"Trial Arena record, arrest warrant, record of time in jail, Commission trial record." Gavya listed off each paper as she picked them up. "Then we have the record of housing and supply placements, an order for bathroom supplies and a lengthy back and forth over what a bathroom needs and how to get it." Everyone chuckled at this, but Gavya continued. "Here is Bella's work record, a notice of failure to appear at work, an IT complaint for a malfunctioning Ward, and finally an arrest warrant for failure to comply with punishment and Ward removal. No record of punishment at all."

"None?" The Avenging Woman asked, glancing over the counter at all the papers.

"None." Gavya replied, firmly.

"It gets worse." Albert stated. He was holding my second arrest record, reading it over. He held it up for everyone to look at. "There is no god's signature on this. Just a seal over where the god's signature should go and Malachi's name."

The Avenging Woman took the warrant out of Albert's hand. She looked it over, her head bobbing as she scanned the paper from the top to the bottom over and over. "This is not valid." The frustration in her was voice palpable. "It must be signed by a god, and not just any god but the one who was responsible for enacting the punishment. From this, I cannot even tell who that should be."

I turned to the Avenging Woman. "How would you know who the god in charge of my punishment should be?"

"It would normally be on the record of punishment form at the end of a trial records, with a certain god assigned to be responsible for making sure the punishment was enacted correctly," she replied. "But your trial was a hung jury left for the humans to decide. That has never been done before. I assume that the Speaker assigned a god to be in charge of enacting your punishment after the humans made their decision and would have recorded that too. But there is no record here from the humans' decision, or from an assignment of responsibility to any god."

I looked at Gavya. "Could that record be somewhere else?"

Gavya shook her head. "All of the records about you, which start with your Trials Arena stuff, were in that box."

"Are there other records about me, or should there be, from before the Trials Arena? Like from when everyone thought I was just a human kid?" I questioned.

Gavya thought about that. "Yes," she finally replied. "There should be a record of that, or at least of your birth. There is a record of every human's birth, death and outcome of their post-death placement." Gavya walked away from the desk, going into the stacks to the left.

After a moment, Gavya's disembodied voice floated back to us. "You were born seventeen years ago, right?"

"Almost eighteen!" I replied. Ben looked at me quizzical and I shrugged, muttering, "I mean, it's true. Eighteen is a big birthday, and I have been seventeen for like a hundred years. You can't blame me if I'm excited about my birthday."

Ben chuckled while Gavya came back to the desk. She had a large three-ring binder in her arms. She plopped it on the desk and flipped through some of the pages. "Your birthday is in March, yes?"

"Yeah, March 23rd." I replied.

Gavya flipped a few pages more, then went one back. "There." She pointed to a spot on the page.

All six of us craned our necks to look at the page at the same time. The page just contained a list of names, followed by dates and times down to the millisecond. Some of them had a second date and time, followed by a place listed. I realized the first date was the date of birth and the second was the date of death. It made me sad to see just how many people born within seconds of me had died already. I noticed a few that even had the birth date and the death date as the same, and one where the birth and death times was only one minute different. The place listed for that person's afterlife was "RE."

"What's RE?" I asked.

Gavya answered me in a hushed tone. "That for a still birth or a human who dies way, way too young. We recycle them, meaning they get a second chance. No one should only get a moment to live and be judged for eternity on that."

That made sense to me, in a sad way, so I stayed quiet. But I kept looking at the page, trying to figure out what Gavya was pointing to. It wasn't my name, so whose was it?

Ben finally spoke. "AnnaBella's name isn't there."

Gavya smiled. "Exactly. A line had been blacked out and instead, it says 'Given Over.' Given Over is used when someone recorded as human at birth is not actually human but will become a god themselves one day. The record of human births has to be amended to reflect the birth of a deity that was not planned. Almost all the gods were present at the formation of everything. But some gods are made gods by the free will of the humans. Sometimes people do certain things in their life in a way that makes the humans decide that they should be a god. Remember our talk about free will? Yeah, this is one of those spots where free will interferes with the Heka's control."

"Wait," I said. "I know we talked about free will and everything, but isn't the Heka, as the maker of everything ever everywhere, like, omnipotent or something?"

Albert chuckled at this. "After everything you have seen and heard, you still think there is anything that could be actually omnipotent the way humans believe omnipotence works?"

I sat back and pouted a little. I guess Albert was right. Clinging to any idea of omni-anything was kind of silly at this moment. Omnipotence and omniscience were right out the window. Maybe the Heka could be omnibenevolent still, but, aw hell. If It is, that would probably suck because that means It would forgive all the gods who did all this stuff and I really, really wanted some justice done.

Gavya and the others ignored my pouting. She continued to explain, "The Heka can't be omnipotent in a world with free will, so It couldn't foresee those gods existing as such. So, It couldn't pre-make them, or sometimes their human birth is so integral to their becoming a god that the Heka couldn't pre-make them, even if It knew they would be a god one day.

"This was part of the system that helped screw so much up before the War. It used to happen a lot, but since the Flood receded, any human-borns that were later decided by humans to be gods were not allowed by the Commission to become truly gods anymore. Hence the rule about humans taking the Trials. They just became a helper for the group that believed in them, their defense attorneys in the courtroom of the afterlife or some such thing. You saw them a lot in your work, Bella." Gavya looked at me, and I nodded. I had seen a lot of these helpers who were not gods but just defense attorneys for the humans in my work.

Gavya continued. "But back when it did happen a lot, the human was considered to never have really been human at all, just kind of a god-in-waiting. So, the human record of their birth had to be given over to the record of the gods."

"I'm confused," I told her. "Why does that matter? What does it have to do with me?"

"Oh, damn." Ben exclaimed. "I get it!"

"Get what?" I asked. "What am I missing?"

Ben looked at me, grinning from ear to ear. "At least one human believes you are a god."

I stepped back from Ben, feeling a little overwhelmed and, if I am honest, scared. Me? A god? "How?" I asked him "And, so what?"

"I don't know the how, but the so what is that this means that the gods know that you now count as a god yourself. You have taken the Trials." Ben reached past Gavya and pulled up my records from the Trials Arena. "And according to this, passed well enough to be allowed to become a god. Then, your record as a human birth was given over to the records of the gods, meaning at least one human believes in you as a god, and has started worshipping you as such. A plus B equals you are a god, with all the rights and responsibilities of one. You are, in fact, a part of the Commission of the Gods now."

Ben paused before he continued, letting this new information sink in. When he spoke again, he seemed antsy. "When did this happen is the bigger question. Did it happen before you were made to act as a coordinator or after? Was this the decision of the humans? To decide the hell with what the Speaker allowed and just to make you a god by a sheer act of will on their part? Because they could, you know. They have that right to overthrow the Commission's decrees and make someone who has taken the Trials, and passed at a god level, a god. If so, if that is what the humans did, somebody has a lot of explaining to do. They defied the absolute will of the humans about their gods."

Gavya continued where Ben left off. "I believe that this means that the humans' decision was to not accept the Speaker's two choices. They rejected the finite choice of making you either a coordinator or a human and chose instead that they would follow the advice of the Trials Arena and make you a god. As a god, the seclusion of you to either the realm of Taikarlu or the realm of the humans became moot. That means there was no reason to Ward you, no reason to separate you from your human form, and no reason at all for your current arrest warrant."

"But this is all just us assuming." Albert took up the thought. "To prove it one way or another, we need the record of the humans' choice after you wrote your story to them. We need that record, but it appears to be missing. Gavya, if that record isn't here, where else could it be?"

"Nowhere," Gavya replied, dismayed. "Here in the Annex is the only place records are sent when they are finished being made."

That thought that had been brewing in my mind made me ask, "And who brings the records here?"

Gavya turned to the Avenging Woman. "They do. The Avenging Women bring the records at the behest of Malachi the Good."

Everyone turned and looked at the Avenging Woman. "It was not I who brought the record of AnnaBella Cain to the Annex. Plus, the record was sealed. Malachi seals records before giving them to us to deliver."

"So, Malachi was the last one who might have had access to the record of the humans' choice," I said. "We need to go ask him about it. And I am thinking maybe we need to ask him this with a little Heka truth-telling pressure. Do you agree, Avenging Woman?"

The Woman nodded.

The decision made, the six of us gathered the paperwork and unsealed box, and walked out of the Annex. At the door, the Avenging Woman in charge told the five surrounding the building to hold their position, letting no one in the Annex except Gavya. Even if another Avenging Woman gave an order for someone else to be let in, they were not to move until she herself came to relieve them, or until Gavya was back in her place at the Annex desk.

As we walked back to the Central Hub in the still empty streets, I asked the Avenging Woman why she did this.

"There is something wrong here," she answered me. "I do not know what, but someone has tampered with the records, and they have also tampered with my work as an Avenging Woman. This I will not stand for. My job is to protect Taikarlu, uphold its laws and keep worship of all the gods fair for the humans. Someone is keeping me from doing my job. I do not know how deep it goes, and if there are other Avenging Women assisting them, I do not want them getting rid of the evidence of their crimes before I find it and bring them to justice for the damage they have done."

"You are an honorable person, Avenging Woman," I told her.

"My name is Ola." The Avenging Woman told me. I actually felt bad that I had never considered that the Avenging Women had names.

"You are an honorable woman, Ola." I corrected myself.

"Thank you," Ola replied.

This time, when we entered the Central Hub, nothing stopped us from going straight to the elevators. We went up to floor 333 and exited into an empty waiting room. The eeriness of the situation again impressed itself on me. I had never seen the waiting room devoid of all humans, but now the chairs all sat vacant. Had death stopped on earth as the gods met to deal with me?

We continued through the waiting room, down the hall and through the silver door at the end. We could hear the commotion inside the Commission Room before we opened the door. Someone was screamin

Dad

The Commission Room was fuller than I had ever seen it. Every seat for the gods on the floor of the Commission Room was full, with people standing and shouting, and others sitting in their seats, arms crossed or turned arguing with their neighbors.

The six of us walked down the center aisle and I turned to look up at the balcony. It was just as full, if not fuller, than the floor was. There were coordinators there, and human residents of Taikarlu. They were arguing and just as angry as their god counterparts were.

On the dais at the front of the room, the Speaker was standing with her arms crossed. She looked angry, sad and confused. In the center of the dais, my father was strapped to a wooden board, his legs bound together, and his hands pinned at his side. He had been the one screaming. An Avenging Woman held a whip in her hand menacingly.

Without thinking, I screamed. "Stop! Do not touch him again!" I couldn't see any physical injuries on him but whatever she had been doing must have hurt him to make his scream so loudly we could hear him in the hall.

The room went from deafening to silent instantly. I looked around and realized that everyone, gods, coordinators and humans, were frozen in place. Out of the side of my mouth, I asked Ola "Is this you or me?"

Ola didn't respond and it took me a moment to realize that my order to stop had done this to everyone, including my friends. I took a breath and released them from the control I didn't mean to put on everyone. I did not release the Avenging Woman with the whip, though. I might have been angry with my father for his actions before, but I would not let that Avenging Woman do whatever she had been doing with that whip to make him scream like he had.

Ola spoke now that she was released. "You did this, AnnaBella Cain. You Heka is strong, stronger than any I have ever seen. No wonder the humans made you a god."

I nodded slightly to show her I had heard. For a moment, all I could do is stare at my father. He wasn't bleeding, so I couldn't be sure the whip was actually used. But I had heard him screaming, so someone had hurt him somehow. The idea of someone hurting my dad made me angrier than I realized I could get.

"Someone tell me what the hell is going on here," I seethed. "Speaker, this is your Commission. Why is that Avenging Woman torturing my father?"

"You vanished," the Speaker gasped out. My hold on her had caused her pain that lingered after I let her go. I knew I should be bothered by that, but she was probably the one who had ordered my father to be hurt, so I really didn't care that it hurt her to talk now. "Then your Ward went offline. We needed to know where you were and what happened to you. Malachi said Nick would know where you were if anyone did. The Avenging Woman was compelling him to speak what he knew but Nick wasn't complying."

I growled in anger and forced the Speaker to stop talking again. This time, by just holding up a hand, motioning for silence. Asking for it, more than compelling. I worked hard to not actually put any Heka behind the motion. I walked over to Dad. As I got closer, I could see that even though he wasn't bleeding, Dad was sweating profusely, and his face was contorted in pain. "Let him go," I told the Avenging Woman.

The Avenging Woman made no moves to act. Ola spoke up, "AnnaBella, she cannot." Oh yeah, my Heka force. I dropped my Heka off the Avenging Woman so she could do as I told her.

The Avenging Woman looked at Ola, who nodded her head for my command to be followed. The Woman then began unstrapping

Dad's arms and legs. He dropped to the floor with a groan, and I ran to him.

"Dad!" I put my arms around him and helped him sit up. "Are you okay?"

Dad looked at me and reached out a trembling arm to stroke my hair. "Bella baby, you're okay. I was so worried about you."

"Dad, I'm fine." I told him, letting him rest against me.

Ben came over with a glass of water and handed it to me. "Drink, Dad," I said and then tipped the glass up to his mouth. Dad took a big gulp of the water and sighed.

"No," Dad replied. "You are not okay. You are angry and you are hurting people because you are angry, Bella. You cannot use your power like this."

"But," I started to say.

Dad sat up straighter, but only fractionally before groaning again. "AnnaBella, I did not teach you to behave like this."

I looked at my father. His face was pained but determined. He was trembling from the pain of whatever they had done to him, but I knew he was right. I couldn't convince everyone I was the one who had been wronged if I used my power this way. Didn't I just decide I would not force sentient beings against their will? I had broken that promise so quickly, just because Dad was hurting. I really needed to learn to control my emotions, and my Heka that seemed to follow them.

I closed my eyes and took a deep breath. My Heka was raging inside me, feeding off my emotions. Calm, I thought. You can be angry but calm. Slowly, my Heka receded back to the cold and warm in my core It usually was. I heard murmuring from the room and knew that my calm was spreading out from me. The gods and coordinators were still wary but not so afraid of me anymore.

I opened my eyes and looked at Dad. He was still trembling. I wanted to deal with the Speaker and everyone who did this to him, but I didn't want to leave him. Ben was still standing next to me and reached his hand down to place it gently on my shoulder.

"I will stay with your dad," Ben said gently. "I will tend to him. Go. Talk to who you need to." He sat down and shifted my dad's weight onto himself.

I let Ben take the weight of Dad and stood up. Reminding myself to stay calm, I moved over to where the Speaker was standing. She seemed very displeased with me.

"Ms. Cain, you cannot just come into my Commission and force your will on everyone like that." She was seething, which I kind of understood, but wasn't going to admit to understanding right now.

"Ms. Speaker," I retorted just as harshly, "you cannot just drag my father in front of your Commission and torture him for information that he did not have and expect me to be happy about it."

The Speaker opened her mouth to respond, but I cut her off with a wave of my hand. Again, I worked really hard to control myself and not exert control over her with my anger-fueled Heka. She could have defied me, but her face said that maybe she knew what she had done was wrong and agreed that she should be chastised for her actions. "You are right. I cannot justify those actions."

"No," I continued. "You can't justify that, no matter how hard you try. In fact, you and I have a lot to talk about. I hope it is a lot that you know nothing about and will be just as shocked to learn as I was. But I can't trust any of the gods right now, including you, so I think the best thing would be for us to go somewhere private to talk and bring Ola with us to make sure everyone stays truthful."

The Speaker nodded tersely. "We can go to my office." She pointed toward the door at the farthest corner of the Commission Room and began walking. I followed, motioning for Ola to come too. Ola got the hint and caught up with me quickly.

Keeping a pace or two behind the Speaker, I spoke quietly with Ola. "When I was in the jail writing my story, an Avenging Woman kept her hand on my shoulder to make me tell the truth as I wrote what I had thought and felt. Can you do that to someone listening? Make their facial expressions and whatever tell the truth of their emotions? Is that something you can do to gods? Is it something a god would agree to having done?"

Ola cocked her head to one side. "If an Avenging Woman places their hand on you, god or no god, your whole body is compelled to tell the truth. I believe facial expressions while listening would be included in that, though I have never used it that way. And every god that is part of the Commission has agreed to Avenging Women being allowed to do this, so they have already given their consent at one point. I do not know why they would rescind their consent now."

"Good," I told Ola. "Do it, if the Speaker agrees. When we get in the office, place your hand on the Speaker's shoulder and just let me do the talking." I stopped for a moment and considered the Speaker's point of view. "In fact, why don't you place a hand on both of our shoulders? That way we both can believe each other."

Ola nodded and replied, "I think that is fair and wise, AnnaBella. I will do as you wish."

The Avenger, The Speaker, & Me

Reaching the door, the Speaker placed a thumb on the door handle and a click sounded. The door swung inward, revealing a moderately sized office. Commanding the center of the room was a large oak desk. Two wing-back chairs covered in crushed gray velvet sat in front of the desk, and a comfortable looking black leather office chair with padded arm rests sat behind it. Behind the chair was a wall of bookshelves. Instead of books, the shelves held an assortment of wood carvings. Some of the carvings were painted and some were plain wood, but all of them were intricately detailed busts of a woman bearing a resemblance to the Speaker. I figured the carvings must have been totems from her human worshippers. They looked really interesting, and I hoped that we could sort all this stuff out and find that she was not part of the bad people, so someday I could come back here and ask the Speaker all about them.

Ola gestured to the wing-back chairs and suggested we sit in those so she could put a hand on both of us at the same time to maintain the honesty of this conversation. The Speaker agreed and we took our seats.

Once Ola had settled a hand on our shoulders and seemed comfortably positioned, I told the Speaker, "I am going to tell you everything. Ola here will ensure you know I am telling the truth, but almost all of it we can back up with documentation from the Annex. What we can't, you will understand why when I finish. Then you can tell me what you were doing to my dad."

"I agree to those terms. But if I find your story lacking, what I do when you are done telling it will be my choice, not your demand." The Speaker straightened herself under Ola's hand.

I nodded my agreement and told her everything. I started from the moment I left the Commission Room after my trial, told her everything about writing my story and then waiting for what felt like ages for a response. I told her about being Warded, being put to work and not being allowed to use the Heka to access the information I needed to do my job. I told her about Gavya, about studying with her. Then I told her about my human memories of waking up in a hospital, my father dead, and my body doing crazy things and passing out.

The more I talked, the more intently the Speaker listened. When I told her about my human self and my coordinator self crossing when I was unconscious, her mouth fell open in surprise. When I told her about Nummi helping remove the Ward and my spirit and body joining back together, the Speaker seemed shocked but kept listening. When I told her about the sealed box and the papers we found inside it, and the ones we didn't, the Speaker seemed to get angry. "So," I finished my story, "when I came into the Commission Room and found you allowing my father to be what at least seemed to me to be tortured at the behest of Malachi the supposedly Good, you can understand why I was angry."

As I had told my story to the Speaker, I realized that a lot of the assumptions we had made in Ben's living room really didn't add up. Maybe the gods did do all that stuff before the Flood. Maybe that was the gods still, but it no longer made sense that the gods were the ones who had broken the rules about me. The only ones who would have really had the access to do all of that would have been the Speaker and Malachi. The Speaker could have ordered Malachi to not follow what the humans said, and to do everything else, but then she would have just assigned herself as the god in charge of my punishment and signed all the paperwork. But no god had signed the paperwork, only

Malachi.

Plus, the Speaker seemed genuinely shocked at what I was telling her. This made it clear to me who really had done everything to prevent me from becoming a god, and I told the Speaker as much. "At this point, everything I know points to that Malachi is the one who hid or destroyed the report on the humans' decision to make me a god. Instead, he chose to have me ripped apart, my body and my spirit, confined them to two different places and, in effect, tried to murder me. For what reason, I don't know."

I sat back and swallowed hard. I had been talking non-stop for what felt like hours. The Speaker also sat back in her chair, her face a confusion of emotions. She looked up at Ola, asking, "Can you remove your hand for a moment and let me process my private thoughts privately? This was a lot to take in."

Ola looked at me and I nodded. The Speaker had obviously not known most of this information, so I could trust her. She deserved a minute to compose herself without her every thought known. Ola removed her hands from us both and the Speaker turned away from me.

After a few minutes, the Speaker turned back towards me. "Please," she gestured towards Ola, who placed her hand back on the Speaker's shoulder. Then, to me, she said "I want you to know I had no part in what was done to you. Malachi was responsible for recording the humans' answer and enacting that. I never considered that they would choose a third option of you becoming a god. If you were made coordinator, your body was to die and be removed, discreetly but respectfully cared for. Your mother was to be told that you would be staying in Taikarlu permanently. I trusted Malachi and never thought I should actually see the record from the humans myself. I just trusted his verbal report to me that you were to be made a coordinator. I assigned a god to fill out the proper punishment forms and amend your court records. I think it was Datin I assigned. I doubt he ever knew. I doubt Malachi ever told him. He just made up his own punishment, a murderous one. Why? Why would Malachi do that?" The longer she spoke, the angrier the Speaker became.

"I have to ask, Speaker," I interjected. "What side did you take in the war?"

The Speaker chuckled, sarcastically. "Me? I did not take a side. I sat in my area of the heavens, guided my people the best I could, and let the bigger gods decide. I see now the mistake that was, but at the time, I thought this was not an issue for such a lowly thing as me. My small tribe of less than one hundred worshippers were just on the brink of moving from cave dwelling to huts. I visited them often, but never dreamed of more. I did not want anything big, just my people left in peace. The Heka never bothered me, but neither did the power the other gods fought for. So, I sat on the sidelines, happy in my own little world."

The Speaker sighed, a tiredness showing in her body, on her face. "Then the Flood came and everything changed. When the waters receded, I found my people again relatively unharmed. So, again, I did not care. I just went back to business as usual. The new rules came and went. Speakers came and went. I did not care. Then, many years ago, I was voted Speaker. I did not ask for it. I did not want it. But I have served the best I could, just waiting for the day I could go back and just be with my people." The Speaker was wistful while talking about her small tribe of worshippers. Something in the way she spoke told me that, even without Ola's hand on her shoulder, I could believe that all she ever wanted was to just be with her people. She was a loving and attentive god, I can tell, I thought to myself.

But then the Speaker kept talking, and she was no longer wistful but full of hurt. "I trusted Malachi to teach me what I needed to serve in my position well. I trusted him, and now I believe he has led me astray. He is the only one who could do this." The Speaker's face contorted. "Now that I think about it. The Heka trusted Malachi too. The only one who could have led the Heka astray during the war and the Flood was Malachi. Maybe even before the war."

I asked the Speaker what she meant.

"Malachi is not a god, but a human. He is a human who was so good in his life in the human realm that he was rewarded by his deity with life everlasting in Taikarlu a long, long time ago. He wasn't the only human ever granted such a thing. It was rare and happened only a handful of times. He and the others like him are not dead, and will never die, but they are not like you were with human needs. Their human bodies are held in suspension in the human realms by Heka power, allowing them to just exist as if no time had ever passed for their human selves. Their resting places are guarded so they cannot be found by humans."

The Speaker seemed to weigh her words, thinking. "Each of them was given a special place here in Taikarlu, and a special job. The others chose to work closely with their personal gods, or the coordinators that worked with their gods. But soon after he came here, Malachi had somehow become friends with the corporeal form of the Heka. It was thought odd, but no one seemed to doubt it then, or put much thought into the oddness of it. Because he was so good, and because he was not a god or a coordinator, the Heka, in Its corporeal form, trusted Malachi completely in a way It could never trust anyone else. The Heka was the one who amended Malachi's god's reward and gave Malachi the power of perception to do the job he does now, as a reward for their friendship. Malachi chose the job of deciding the true faiths of the humans himself. Actually, he created it, with the Heka's help. There were so many faiths, some of them worshipping the same god or gods but with very different rules, so this position became needed.

"The Heka also gave Malachi the power to build the jail, and create the Avenging Women, at Malachi's suggestion, so they would have a way to punish the gods who had defied the Heka when the war was won. He was so sure that the Heka could win and was so heartbroken when the corporeal Heka vanished after the Floods, everyone just let him carry on doing his job and being the leader of the Avenging Women after the Joint Commission got re-founded and set to work figuring out how we gods should behave."

The Speaker stopped, thinking for a long while. When she spoke again, her words took on a new determination, a new anger. It almost felt like betrayal. "If you and your friends are right about what happened, that the Heka was trapped in the jail and that is what cause the Floods, then it must have been Malachi, not the gods opposing the Heka, who convinced the Heka to go into the jail. It must have been Malachi who tricked the Heka and has held It bound this whole time. Although I don't know how or where he would have hidden the Heka."

I nodded. The Speaker was right. It must be Malachi.

"I am so sorry, Ms. Cain. I am sorry for what I did to your father. Malachi convinced me your father had to know where you were, that you broke the laws and would never leave without telling him. I trusted him, just as the Heka trusted him. I should have been more suspicious. I should have tried another way first. Malachi was just..." The Speaker slammed a fist onto the armrest of her chair in frustration. "He was just so damn convincing."

"It's not your fault, Ms. Speaker," I replied kindly. "Apparently, Malachi the Good convinced a lot of people to do a lot of things against their better judgement. Malachi the Good ain't all that good after all. We need to confront him about all this and force him to tell us what really happened."

With no warning, Ola stood up straight and said "Malachi the Good is never wrong. Malachi the Good cannot be questioned. Malachi the Good is the Good."

The Speaker and I looked at each other with concern. I had seen this action before in the lobby but she hadn't. Malachi must have programmed the Avenging Women when he made them to defend him at all costs. The fact that he did that led more credence to the idea that not only did Malachi at least plan to do something wrong before he ever even made them, but that he knew what he was planning to do was very, very wrong. How could we force Malachi to talk to us and confront our accusations if he had somehow programmed the Avenging Women to always defend him?

The Speaker stood and placed both her hands on Ola's shoulders. "No, Avenging Woman. Malachi the Good is not always good. He is a man. Malachi is not even a god, but just a very old man. He was good in his life and was given the reward to never die. But that does not mean he will always be good. Even the best people can turn and do bad things if there is enough motivation for it."

Ola still stood straight, not looking directly at the Speaker. "Malachi the Good is never wrong. Malachi the Good cannot be questioned," she began but before she could finish, the Speaker slapped her across the face.

"Avenging Woman!" the Speaker yelled. "I am the Speaker of the Commission. I declare emergency at the highest level. Malachi is to be found and brought before me. He is to be treated as an enemy of the gods of the highest order. He is not good, but a criminal by order of the Speaker. Do you understand?"

Ola still did not look at the Speaker, only repeating "Malachi the Good is never wrong. Malachi the Good cannot…"

What were the Avenging Women and how did Malachi create them in this way that stopped them from using their own free will? I didn't have an answer to how he made them, but my mind went back to my discussion with Gavya about free will. "Even if the Heka made something, then made the gods out of that something, it would still have free will as a part of it," I remembered her telling me. It was a safe bet that Malachi would not realize that if he made a sentient being out of anything Heka made that, no matter how he programmed it, he wouldn't have been able to prevent the free will from slipping in too.

This gave me an idea. I stood and faced the Avenging Woman myself, speaking softly. "Ola. Use your free will. Malachi is not good. Ola, hear me, please."

Ola just kept speaking. "…be questioned. Malachi the Good is the Good. Malachi the Good is never wrong. Malachi the Good cannot be questioned. Malachi the Good is the Good."

Not knowing what else to do, I reached inside of me to my Heka and forced all of it that I could at Ola. "No! Malachi is Not Good!" I pushed this thought at Ola with all my might. I didn't force her to believe it, or I tried really hard not to. I just pushed her to remember she had the free will to decide to believe me if she wanted to.

Ola stumbled back, shaking her head. She looked at me with tears in her eyes. "AnnaBella, I can't. I can't stop. Help me."

"You just did, Ola," I told her, and took her hands into mine. "You just did. You stopped. Do you believe me? Do you believe me when I tell you that we have evidence that Malachi may not be good, but actually did something very wrong?"

Ola nodded that, yes, she believed me.

"Good," I told her. "Now we need to get all the other Avenging

Women to as well, and get Malachi in front of the Commission to tell the truth."

Ola squeezed my hands, sobs escaping her that she tried to subdue. It was odd to see such a powerful being cry, but all I could do was keep holding her hands and pretend it wasn't weird. Slowly, Ola regained her composure fully and was once again the powerful being we were all used to seeing. She radiated justice, but this time I didn't feel it directed at me.

The Speaker reiterated her statement. "Malachi should be brought before the Commission on an emergent status, for threatening the safety of the gods. All rights and special treatment he receives as a human in Taikarlu are temporarily suspended until he can be tried for the crimes charged against him, on the order of the Speaker. Spread the word to all the other Avenging Women. If there is not a law that covers this that you can quote to overcome the issues they may have, I hereby make one, also on emergent status, that no human can outrank the Speaker during a state of emergency in Taikarlu. And I now declare us in a state of emergency. Does that cover everything?"

"I believe so," Ola whispered.

The Speaker said "Then go," tersely and Ola left the office. As soon as the door shut behind Ola, the Speaker sank into a wing-back chair, putting her head in her hands. "Why on my watch? Why did all this have to come out on my watch?"

"Because you are the only one that cared enough to listen, I think." I told her. "Why did the Heka choose to talk to me from Its confinement? Why did It ask me to free It? Why now? I think because It knew that now It could. I would question things. You would listen to my questions."

The Speaker breathed heavily. "I guess we should go back out there and inform the whole of Taikarlu what is going on. They all came because no one had ever defied our justice system before and it was a novelty. Now, they are in for a real treat. Rather than seeing me punish an absconder, they will see me punish a traitor."

Everybody from Everywhere

The Speaker and I made our way back out to the Commission Room floor. The gods, coordinators, and other Taikarlu residents were milling around, talking to one another and didn't notice our return. But Nummi did and flagged us over to the table where they were sitting. My father had apparently felt well enough to move to a chair and was sitting up, looking much better than he had when I left.

"Dad." I said to him. "Are you okay?"

Dad reached his hand out to me, and I took it. I did not like how weak his grip was. "I will be fine, Bella." I hoped he wasn't lying.

"What were they doing to you?" I asked. "You aren't bleeding or anything, but the Avenging Woman had a whip."

Dad sighed. "You have felt what it is like when an Avenging Woman puts you under arrest, and what it is like when they compel you to tell the truth. Have you ever felt what it is like when you don't tell the truth under that compulsion? When you purposefully lie?"

I nodded that I had. While writing my story for the humans to judge me by, I had tested that power of compulsion just to show the humans I wouldn't lie about anything. It was less than pleasant, to say the least.

"That's what the whip does," Dad told me. "It makes their compulsion believe you are lying even when you are not, or at least not telling them the whole truth. You feel the pain of lying, even when telling the truth."

Why would they ever need that, I thought. That's just torture. If their mere presence, if just touching you makes you tell the truth, and lying makes you feel pain, why would they ever need a weapon that made you feel pain when you told the truth too? That's just cruel.

Before I could say anything, the Speaker knelt down beside Dad. "I must apologize for my actions. I was led astray into thinking that you had information with no real evidence to say you did. I did, or rather allowed to be done, horrible things to you. I am sincerely sorry for my actions. I will do everything I can to make it right, starting with removing your punishment for having a child with a human."

Dad swallowed some water and answered. "Thank you, Ms. Speaker. I believe that you were acting with the best of intentions, even if those intentions were led to conclusions falsely. I am just happy my daughter is safe. You are safe, aren't you?"

"Yes, Dad." I replied. "Well, reasonably. I may have accidentally broken an Avenging Woman, discovered a traitor in Taikarlu and figured out who started the Great War and caused the Flood, but I am reasonably safe and okay."

Dad's eyes went wide and he choked on his water. "You broke an Avenging... AnnaBella Cain, what have you done?"

The Speaker answered for me. "The right thing, Dad. Don't worry. She has done the right thing." With that said, the Speaker walked to the center of the floor and clapped her hands to bring everyone to attention. Dad continued to eye me suspiciously, in a way that would normally mean I was probably being grounded, but eventually he turned away from me and looked at the Speaker. I don't know that Dad really could ground me now if he wanted to. I kind of out-rank him. That thought made me smile a little. At some point, I realized, I was going to have to tell Dad, that, sorry, I'm not going to be a coordinator like you, but a god. Oh, jeez, I'm a god. Is that weird to think about? Yep. Very weird. Very, very weird.

When everyone finally settled down, the Speaker spoke loudly. "I have something to say." She cleared her throat and began again. "Taikarlu has been put in a state of emergency. Evidence has been brought before me that someone has been overthrowing the orders and decisions of this court. This person has been actively working to

181

undermine the order and safety of our land and potentially had something to do with the disappearance of the physical form of the Heka. The Avenging Women are on a mission to bring that person to us here, to be tried for the crimes of being a traitor and a terrorist. I would ask that everyone stay here, in the Commission Room, until they return with Malachi the Good."

As the Speaker talked, the gods and coordinators became visibly more and more agitated. At the mention of Malachi the Good, the room erupted. People began yelling that there was no way Malachi was a traitor, that someone else must be to blame. The Speaker held up her hands to get silence again and settled for quiet, disgruntled murmurs.

"Everyone," she said calmly, "the evidence is there. I would not make these allegations lightly, especially not against one so trusted as Malachi. Please, we have a system for dealing with alleged criminal behavior and part of that system is that we all be as unbiased as we can. I know it will be hard, but a fair trial needs to happen. Not just when we dislike someone but also when they are beloved. Please be patient and let the Avenging Women do their job so that we can do ours as swiftly as possible and put this whole thing behind us."

The murmurs continued but no one yelled out again. Everyone stayed in the Commission Room and waited, as asked. I stayed with Dad, giving him a rundown of everything I knew and assuring him over and over that I was fine. Nummi and Albert wandered off at some point. I saw them talking with a few of the other gods and assumed they were catching up with old friends. Ben stayed with me and Dad, refilling Dad's water occasionally and adding details to my story. Gavya sat at the table next to Dad, clutching the pile of papers we had brought from the Annex for dear life, looking lost in the big crowd.

After what felt like an eternity, the doors of the Commission Room burst open and four Avenging Women came through them. Behind them, his arms holding on to two more Avenging Women, was Malachi. Four more Avenging Women trailed in after him. Malachi appeared old and frail but was moving under his own power. I guessed that the breaking of his spell over the Avenging Women only worked so well.

When he reached the dais of the Speaker, Malachi asked in an innocent voice "What's this all about?"

The Speaker pointed to the defendant's table. "Malachi, please take a seat. You have been accused of conspiring to subvert the rules and justice of this land and of being a traitor to the Heka. You must face a trial of the gods. Would you like an advocate?"

"No, no," Malachi answered. "I have done nothing." He walked over to the defendant's table and sat down.

The Speaker looked slightly confused. "Normally, I would ask you to declare a person's chosen faith at this time. Are you willing to share yours, or should I?" She trailed off for a moment, then continued. "Um, well, I guess your faith does not matter at this point. If you are innocent, we don't need to know it. If you are guilty, then the punishment will be the same no matter your gods. Full death and evisceration of the soul."

"What do you believe I did, Ms. Speaker?" Malachi asked, his voice watery and weak sounding.

Before she could speak, I stood up. "Ms. Speaker, sorry to interrupt, but wouldn't this be easier if we just used the Avenging Women and asked him? I mean, if he can produce the record from the humans, and it showed he did what they said to do, all this could be over with no trial at all, right? If he can't, then we need a trial to figure out what really happened and if really was the cause."

The Speaker nodded. "Right, Ms. Cain. Avenging Women, can you lay your hand on Malachi please? We need a truthful answer from him."

One Avenging Woman stepped up and placed her hand on Malachi's right shoulder.

The Speaker then asked, "Malachi, where is the record of the humans' choice in the matter of the punishment of AnnaBella Cain?"

"There isn't one." Malachi stated, the weakness suddenly gone from his voice,

The Speaker then asked, "Then how was the method of her punishment decided?"

"I decided." Malachi spat out. "The brat was born without

permission. She was supposed to be punished but the humans were deciding to make her a god for nothing. She did nothing and gets to be a god? Bah! The Heka talks to her and fixes her mistakes, and she gets honored while I live my human life in abject poverty, doing everything right and all I get for a reward is infinite servitude?" Malachi turned from facing the Speaker to face the crowd in the rest of the room. "You couldn't even make me young again? Or handsome? No! Just live forever, Malachi. Serve forever, Malachi. Hobble around with arthritis and no teeth and aches and pains as a reward, Malachi!"

"Enough!" The Speaker cut Malachi off. Then she looked down at her lap and muttered to herself. "I have to ask. I have to." She looked up and spoke clearly again. "Malachi, did you have anything to do with the disappearance of the Heka in physical form?"

"Hah!" Malachi laughed. "I didn't have just something to do with it, I did it alone, myself!"

The room exploded again with shouting. Some were yelling that this wasn't a fair trial, where is the evidence they were promised, who had corrupted the Avenging Women? Others gasped and cried at the realization that their favorite human may not be the pinnacle of goodness they had assumed him to be, and how could he do such a thing as make the Heka disappear.

The Speaker fought for silence again and, again, gave up and called it good enough when the noise level got low enough that we could hear her. "Malachi, I can feel your anger in your responses, which are a little too forthright and honest. Perhaps you would not be saying so much if the hand of the Avenging Woman was not upon you."

Malachi laughed again and pushed the hand of the Avenging Woman off his shoulder. "The fact that the Avenging Women dared arrest me tells me you know more than I ever wanted you to. The game is up for me, no matter how you slice it. The punishment for what I have done is total death of my body, spirit and soul, so why not just admit to what I have done? You said it yourself, Speaker, the punishment for being a traitor to the gods is evisceration of the soul." He spit those last words out like they were poison in his mouth.

The Speaker's mouth opened as if she would respond, anger and shock on her face, but Malachi did not give her a chance. "If I am going down, I am taking all of you with me. You think you are so righteous, you gods. You think because you have abilities given to you by the Heka, you have the right to decide everything for us humans. How we live, how we die, how we spend eternity, it is all in your hands. Sometimes you care, and control everything. Sometimes, you don't and everything in our world goes to hell. But it is only that way because you made it that way."

"The Heka set up this world. It decided these things, not us," the Speaker said quietly. I could tell that she probably wanted to yell and shake Malachi, but, somehow, she was containing all those feelings.

At this, Malachi really did spit, right on the Commission Room floor. "The Heka? The Heka is a feckless power that gave everything away to make the gods. It gave all Its power to you and what did you do with it? Fought for more. There was never enough power to appease any of you. Look at any text, any one of them. For years, you gods played your games, controlling the world. Our world. Do this, don't do that, I am walking beside you, helping you, giving you everything you need. Then you just quit. The power games here became more fun."

Malachi walked out, away from the table, into the Commission room floor, turning to look at everyone. He spread his arms wide, as if including everyone in his condemnation. "So, you abandoned us, your people, who had no idea how to live without you. You left us with creatures of your own making, and no power to control them. You tore our world apart and then just walked away. The Heka made Itself have a physical form to try and undo the damage you did. Instead of listening, you fought It. You fought your own wars over who should be in charge and ignored the wars you created in us."

Malachi barely stopped to breath during his rant. The Commission Room had finally gone silent as everyone listened to his accusations. "When I saw what was happening, I realized I was the only one with any power to stop it. I created Wards to control the children of the gods that were ravaging the human realm. The Heka was so impressed with me, then. It was pleased I figured out a solution for the problem It allowed, that It befriended me, listened to me, confided in me. Then, I dropped a hint here, make a quiet suggestion there, and boom, the Heka was convinced to let me build a place where the Heka Itself could not work. A jail, I built, but It didn't even know why. You gods thought you could use it to suppress your enemies. Gods used Wards to trick each other to go into the jail but be free to leave it themselves, thinking they could use my creations to help them gain more power. But you never knew my creations' real purpose: to contain the Heka's form and make your world go to hell the way mine had. When your world was torn apart, then you cared. But by then, it was too late."

Malachi held up his right arm, showing off a scar similar to mine. "Do you think I would just create the jail and the Wards without giving myself the ability to not be controlled by someone else using my creations? Of course, I wasn't that stupid. I Warded myself, with a special Ward. I was able to go inside that jail while the rest of you languished in eternal waters. I took the Heka and put It in a cage, another creation of my own making. This cage allows the Heka's spirit out so that everything can function, but left all of you feeling bereft. The insatiable power you once had was limited. Now you had to share. But you had to share in a place that was no longer immeasurable. You had to deal with death and destruction, the same as you made the humans deal with. Your favorite pet monsters, unicorns and mystical beings were gone, missing. How did it feel to see your world change and have to struggle to fix it on your own? You were abandoned, just like you abandoned us."

Malachi laughed, a maniacal laugh. "It is out there, in the Wastes. The Heka has been out there the whole time. It cried out to be saved but you all were so busy trying to make this place perfect again, you didn't listen. Then comes AnnaBella Cain, she asked too many annoying questions. And she had power, too much power. Somehow, she was powerful enough to reach out to the Heka and talk to It."

Malachi turned towards me, lowered his tone and seemed resentful. "Ms. Cain, you think you are a victim in this, but you are not. You are like me. You saw that the humans are better without the gods at all. But in your naivety, I saw a growing belief in you that the Heka's return could fix things. I saw you start to believe that the Heka should be brought back in Its corporeal form. I knew It was talking to you, guiding you on how to find It. I could not let you bring It back. I thought the humans would see that too, that the world would not be better under the Heka, but without any gods at all. They failed me. They believed in you and failed me. So, I had to destroy you before anyone else knew."

Malachi shook his head and spoke again, the venom in his voice returning. He clenched his fists and slammed them on the table. "But then you got smart and figured out the whole game! Damn you and your too smart, too nosy, loud mouth!" His eyes started rolling and foam formed at the corners of his mouth. "You will never save It. Never! I hid them. Ten keys to unlock the Heka and I hid them where you will never find them. The Heka is dying, Its soul separated from Its spirit for too long, no body at all for too long, and you can't do anything about it. Nothing. The Heka was foolish to ever make a body. Bodies have spirits and souls. Gods only have spirits. Their bodies are fake, an illusion, so they don't have souls. But the Heka went and made Itself a real body, not an illusion of one. Once It made Itself a body, It went from just a soul to having, and needing, all three: the body, soul and spirit. It became bound to all three."

Malachi walked closer to me. "You know what it feels like, AnnaBella Cain. You know. When your body and spirit are separated for too long, the pain, the sickness that happens then. You know that death eventually follows. The Heka lasted longer because It was so strong, but Its time is running out. There is no body anymore for It to return to. I destroyed Its body. But I trapped Its soul. Its spirit is out there, wandering somewhere, but the soul is trapped, dying. When the Heka dies, so do all of you. So does everything! Hahaha! No one knows where I hid the mystical beings that hold the keys to Its cage. And I will never tell, never!" Malachi started laughing, a deep, maniacal laugh that had even the Avenging Women stepping back away from him.

Out of nowhere, a flaming ball fell off the balcony and rolled down the aisle. It took me a moment to realize that the flaming ball actually didn't fall or roll, but jumped and ran. It was Bob. He ran, screaming and covered from head to toe in flames. Little sparks fell off him and singed the carpet, leaving a trail of burn marks along his path to Malachi.

"Where is It?" Bob screamed. He grabbed Malachi by the arms and started shaking him. "Where is the Heka? How could you do this? You were my friend! You were my devotee. You left me food every day on your altar, and I always blessed you for it. Always! I never forgot you. And this is how you repay me? This! I haven't touched another person in thousands of years because of you! Where is the Heka?"

Malachi's clothes were burning from Bob's touch, but Malachi just laughed more. "You blessed me? You won't let me die. You won't cure my pains but won't let me die. You call this a reward? Burn forever, you heartless bitch of a god!" Malachi laughed again.

Bob stepped back away from Malachi, who was mostly naked now and his arms had huge burn marks in the shape of Bob's hands. I turned to Ben and asked him what they meant.

Ben whispered, "Bob used to be a god, Malachi's god. Bob was the one who rewarded Malachi with eternal life in Taikarlu for his faithful worship and service. He also gave his people the coffee plant as a reward for their hard work. The bush grew in many places, but only thrived in a few, and was later discovered by Ethiopian monks but that is another story. But then, Bob changed, and no one knew why. He burned unless he had caffeine. We all thought it was a punishment from the Heka for giving caffeine to humans, kind of like the whole, thing with Prometheus and fire. I guess, maybe not, though. Maybe Malachi cursed Bob because he didn't like his reward. Anyway, all of Bob's worshippers became scared of him and abandoned him, so he got stuck working in Finance like a coordinator. He was stripped of his godhood and everything, because we thought he was being punished."

I didn't respond to Ben, but I thought maybe Malachi has a little bit of a point there. What kind of reward is it to suffer every day in pain and be told that you should be happy about it? Sounds a little gaslighting to me, but to make Bob burn forever for it? Maybe Malachi should have tried talking to Bob first.

Malachi had continued raving while Ben was talking. "You will never stop burning. Never. Only the Heka can stop my curse and the Heka will die. Everything will die, Bob, but you? You will still be alive, in the nothingness left behind, burning. That is my curse I gave you. A gift for a gift, some faiths believe, including the one you made. A gift for a gift, Bob. You gave me the gift of torture in paradise, so I gave you the same gift in return."

As Malachi laughed, Bob grew angrier. His flames grew white, then blue. His flames were so intense it hurt to look at him. He screamed "I loved you!" Then Bob stunned everyone by grabbing Malachi in a bear hug.

At first, Malachi just kept laughing. But slowly, his laughter turned to screams. As we watched, Bob's intense flames burned Malachi. His body dissolved into ash in Bob's arms. Malachi's screams faded away but Bob kept standing there, holding nothing, his flames too bright to look at.

No one spoke. Time crawled by as we all watched Bob clutch the nothingness that used to be Malachi and cry. Slowly, Bob's flames dimmed back to white, then orange, and then red. Finally, Bob burned his anger and sadness out. When he was only smoking, an Avenging Woman finally risked taking him by the arm and leading him out of the Commission Room, still crying and holding piles of ash.

No one spoke for the longest time. I looked around the Commission Room and saw everyone, all the gods, coordinators and humans all just staring at the spot where Bob and Malachi had been. All that remained was a charred spot on the purple carpet.

Finally, the Speaker cleared her throat, bringing everyone's attention back to her. There was a moment of rustling as everyone sat down in their seats. When that was done the Speaker cleared her throat again.

"This," she started. Then she stopped. The room stayed silent, waiting to see what she would say. The Speaker looked at me, then around the room, making eye contact with as many people as she could.

Then she tried again. "Justice was not served here today. Malachi admitted to many things. We will never know how true they all were. Bob will need to be dealt with as well, but in light of the things Malachi said, and the fact that Malachi was still technically Bob's worshipper, we will need to do some research to determine what dealing with Bob means. In the meantime…"

The Heka

The Speaker was still talking but I could not hear her anymore. My ears suddenly started roaring. I rubbed them, hoping to make the sound go away, but it only got louder. I tried to focus on the Speaker, but slowly my vision went hazy. Black spots danced in front of my eyes, growing larger and larger.

Then I heard a voice. "Bella."

It was the Heka talking to me inside my head. I reached out to put my hand on the table in front of me as my world started to swim, but I just kept reaching and reaching. The world had gone away and I was in the deep nothingness again.

Time was gone here. I could feel planets and universes be born and die. I could hear the grass grow. My body was a speck and also larger than the oceans. I was swimming and running and standing still. I finally understood what this place I went to was. It was the Heka's cage. When I was transported to nowhere, I was seeing inside the cage Malachi had trapped the Heka's soul in.

The voice came to me again. "Bella."

"Yes?" I finally found my voice to respond.

"Malachi is right. I am dying. Save me," the Heka called.

"How?" I asked.

"Find me." The Heka's voice felt weak, not so booming as It once had.

"Where?" My mind was buzzing with the fullness and emptiness of the cage. The Heka' s cage was huge. But, now understanding where I was, I could feel the walls of that cage pressing against me. I could feel how trapped, how scared the Heka was in there, alone and lonely. That fear and loneliness was so intense it made me want to cry. I could only answer in one-word sentences and even that was hard.

"Malachi told you where to look. He hid me where no one would find me. He hid the keys to my prison with the mystical beings. There are ten of them. You found one but do not know you did. Gavya knows. Find me." The Heka's voice seemed to be fading fast. It did not have the power to keep this up for much longer, I could tell.

"Yes." I told the Heka. I felt the Heka float away. Or really, I floated away from the Heka. Part of me didn't want to leave It alone there. I wanted to stay, keep It company and not let It die alone. But another part of me knew I didn't have much time. I had to leave It alone for now if I wanted to save It. Stay and keep It company while It died, or leave and let It be lonely while I tried to find It to let It live? I wanted the Heka to live. Everyone needed the Heka to live, so I let go and floated away.

Slowly, the emptiness around me was replaced by sounds of people talking. The feeling of universes was replaced by itchy carpet and rough hands. I was back inside myself and I was not moving, but laying on the floor.

"Bella baby! Damn it, this happens a lot?" I heard Dad saying.

Ben chuckled. "Yeah, she is always embarrassed by it. Just give her a minute, she'll come around."

I groaned. Great, I thought my passing out stuff was done when I put my body and spirit back together. Now I went and did it in front of the entirety of Taikarlu. Just great.

I opened my eyes to see my dad and Ben leaning over me. Behind Ben, the Speaker was pacing nervously. I could hear the murmurings of the residents of Taikarlu in the background.

"Ugh," I groaned again. "How long was I out?"

"About five minutes, that's all." Ben told me.

"Baby girl," Dad placed his hand under my head, cradling me. "Are you okay. Are you hurt? You fell pretty hard." Now I had Dad worrying over me passing out instead of Mom. Double great.

I did my mental checklist of my aches and pains. Everything seemed okay, so I tried to sit up. Dad tried to help me even though I didn't need it. He was the one that was recently tortured. I should have been helping him, not the other way around.

"Ms. Cain?" the Speaker came closer and questioned me. "What happened? You fell and were muttering about the Heka. Did you speak with It again?"

"Yeah," I told her. "Yeah, I spoke with It." I struggled to stand, and Dad tried to help again but honestly, he just made it harder. I shrugged him off and gained my feet.

Dad pulled over a chair and motioned for me to sit in it, but I waved him off. I took a deep breath and spoke loudly, not just to the Speaker but to everyone.

"Malachi wasn't lying. He hid the Heka, and It is now dying. Its power is getting really weak. It could barely talk to me." I told them all.

"What do we do?" The Speaker asked.

I shook my head. "Not we, me. I have to find It. It didn't say this but I think It expects me to do it alone. It said that I have to find the keys to Its prison with the mystical creatures, that I already found one but don't know it. It said Gavya knows."

Gavya had spent this entire time sitting quietly in a corner clutching her papers. She had never been in the Commission Room before and definitely had never experienced it at its fullest. The idea of the whole of Taikarlu staring at her, as they were doing now, scared her witless. At the mention of her name, Gavya looked up, wild terror in her eyes.

"Me?" She squeaked. "I don't know anything."

I walked shakily over to Gavya and placed a comforting hand on her shoulder. "The Heka says you do. You know something, even if you don't think you do. Where are the mystical creatures, Gavya?" I said all of this to her in a low voice meant just for the two of us.

Gavya thought for a moment, her panic at being called out in front of the whole group like this still evident. But then I saw it on her face. She figured it out.

"The oasis," she exclaimed. "There was something hiding in the oasis, remember?"

I nodded to Gavya. I did remember. We both had mentioned that it felt like something was watching us when we swam in the lake. It hadn't felt harmful or malicious so we had ignored it. But what if that thing watching us was a mystical creature with a key?

"Thank you, Gavya," I said quietly. Louder, to the whole Commission Room, I told them "There is an oasis in the Wastes. It is impossible to find if you are looking for it, but not impossible to find if you only are looking for safety. I asked the sand to show me the way, and it did. I can find it again. Gavya believes that a mystical creature may be there, hiding."

Ben spoke up then. "If there is one, there may be more. Ten keys mean probably ten mystical creatures. That means probably ten oases."

"Eleven," Gavya corrected, her voice shaky as she tried to be bold.

"Eleven?" I asked her.

Eleven," she repeated. "Ten keys, ten creatures, ten oases. But one more oasis where the Heka is hidden. Eleven."

The Speaker then took command. "We will give you everything you need, Ms. Cain. Whatever you ask for, we will provide. Will you go into the Wastes for us? Find the Heka and save Its life? Save us all?"

I looked at my father, and then at Ben, Gavya, Nummi and Albert. My friends. My family. Nobody survived the Wastes. But I did, with Gavya. That was only for a short time, though. Could I survive walking in it to find eleven oases, not just one? I was here, in Taikarlu, with a human body, surviving when no one else ever had. Could I do this too?

I decided I had no choice. I had to. The Heka asked me to. The Speaker asked me to. The whole world was asking me to. Who was I to back out now?

"I need," I thought for a bit, then looked at Dad. "I need you to tell Mom. Tell her everything. Then take care of her. I can't do this unless I know she will be okay. Mari is with her, but I think she needs you, Dad."

Dad nodded his head. "I will go to her now, with the Speaker's permission." He looked over at the Speaker, who gave an affirmative wave. "I will stay with her until you are home safe, I promise."

"Thank you," I told him. He came up and hugged me tight for a brief moment, then left the Commission Room.

"What else do you need, dear?" The Speaker asked me.

I thought for a long time. I have a human body like before, but I didn't think I would get hungry or thirsty. My Heka protection seemed to keep all that under control. But maybe I should take things humans would need just in case. I grabbed a piece of paper and started writing everything I could think of down. A tent, food, water, sleeping bags, probably some clothes that are good for the desert. I looked at my list and thought it was probably good enough. I would just have to hope that my Heka would be good enough like I thought to cover anything I forgot. I handed the list to the Speaker, who handed it to a god nearby. That god looked over the list, nodded, and ran off, probably to get the things I had requested. I called out to stop him.

"Get enough of that stuff for more than one person, okay?" I asked.

He nodded once, curtly, then continued on his way.

I looked around at all the expectant faces watching me. Only one didn't have a look of concern. Only one was smiling, and that was Ben.

"I know I said I think I need to go alone," I told him. "But you wanna come anyway?"

Ben's grin grew even wider. "Heck, yeah." He took my arm in his, linked at the elbow. "Let's go on an adventure to save the world."

I cleared my throat and spoke as loudly as I could. "Ms. Speaker, I have no other needs. We will go to the Wastes and find the Heka, Ben and I." Ben pulled me to start walking away, his stride a wide and confident gait, as if he was excited. We walked out of the Commission Room and down the hall.

As the silver door closed behind us, I heard the Speaker saying "Good luck."

About the Author

Kefira Zink is an author from a little town in Michigan. She has a bachelor's degree in Sociology from Arizona State University and a master's degree in Sociology, with a specialty in Religion and Deviance from American Public University. She loves buying books, especially rescuing old books and giving them a loving home as well as reading books (which any reader will tell you, buying books and reading them are two very different hobbies). She is married to her wonderful husband/muse and together they have six grown children, two cats, a dog that thinks it is a cat, and a lizard that thinks it is a dinosaur.

Connect With The Author

Website: https://sites.google.com/view/kefira-zink-author
Email: kefirazinkauthor@gmail.com
Facebook: Kefira Zink Author
TikTok: kefira_zink_author